D0378504

"YOU'RE SERVING BUGS FOR LUNCH!"

A slow smile spread across Miss Larva's face. Her black eyes brightened. "Oh, I see, Fitz! You're enjoying my lunches, are you? Why didn't you just say so?"

The cook stepped aside and waved her hand toward the huge flat pan she had been stirring. It was the largest pan Fitz had ever seen.

He moved cautiously forward to take a closer look. In the pan was a thin layer of reddish sauce with lots of lumpy things swimming around in it.

He gasped and shrank back. "Those are *caterpillars!*" Fitz cried. "You're serving bugs for lunch!"

BONE CHILLERS™

BACK TO SCHOOL

BETSY HAYNES

HarperPaperbacks
A Division of HarperCollins*Publishers*

This is a work of fiction. The characters, incidents, and dialogues are products of the author's imagination and are not to be construed as real. Any resemblance to actual events or persons, living or dead, is entirely coincidental.

HarperPaperbacks *A Division of* HarperCollins *Publishers*
10 East 53rd Street, New York, N.Y. 10022

Copyright © 1994 by Betsy Haynes and
Daniel Weiss Associates, Inc.

Cover art copyright © 1994 Daniel Weiss Associates, Inc.

Bone Chillers is a trademark of Daniel Weiss Associates, Inc.

All rights reserved. No part of this book may be used
or reproduced in any manner whatsoever without written
permission of the publisher, except in the case of brief
quotations embodied in critical articles and reviews.
For information address Daniel Weiss Associates, Inc.,
33 West 17th Street, New York, N.Y. 10011.

Printed in the United States of America.

HarperCollins®, colophon, and HarperPaperbacks™
are trademarks of HarperCollins Publishers, Inc.

Originally published by HarperPaperbacks™. This edition published
by Reader's Digest Young Families, Inc., with the permission of
Daniel Weiss Associates, Inc.

In memory of the real Miss Buggy Webb, my seventh-grade teacher, who taught me about insects in a much nicer way.

Chapter

Fitz Traflon scowled into the trash can. Running across the top of the empty cans and cartons and congealed spaghetti inside was a giant brown cockroach. It was at least as big as Fitz's thumb. He wrinkled his nose in disgust. Then he held the empty peanut-butter jar directly over it.

"Bombs away!" he said as he dropped the jar.

He picked up the jar and looked under it. The cockroach's antennae were still moving. Aiming carefully, he shoved the jar into the garbage as hard as he could. Then he lifted it once more, surveying the now-smushed cockroach with satisfaction.

Most of his friends were fascinated by bugs, but not Fitz. He hated them. He didn't really know why, but he'd been completely disgusted by anything creepy or crawly ever since he could remember.

Grabbing his peanut-butter-and-jelly sandwich from the counter, he stuffed it into his bulging backpack. With his luck it would be as smushed as the cockroach by lunchtime. A brown and purple gooey mess.

"Who cares?" he muttered under his breath. "I can't believe it's my twelfth birthday *and* the first day of school. What a rotten way to celebrate."

As Fitz headed for the back door, his mother looked up from the crossword puzzle she was working at the kitchen table. "Have a nice day, dear," she said cheerily.

"And happy birthday, son," added his father, setting down his coffee cup and smiling at Fitz over the top of the newspaper.

Fitz grunted, then he trudged out of the house and down the sidewalk. He was thinking about past birthdays. Every year until now, his birthday had fallen a day or two before the start of school. It had been an awesome way to celebrate the end of summer vacation—his parents always took him and a group of his friends to the amusement park or some other fun place. But today the only place he was going was to school. Ugh.

He was still grumbling to himself when he arrived at Maple Grove Middle School. He stopped on the sidewalk and looked up at the two-story redbrick building. It looked just like it had last year.

Like a prison.

Fitz sighed and shoved his hands into his pockets. He hated school. Every year it was the same old stuff—except that every year it got harder and harder. He had hoped all summer that this year things would change—that school would be fun, maybe. Or at least different somehow.

But as he stared at the familiar grim front of the school building, he had a sinking feeling that he was going to be out of luck.

"Hi, Fitz! Guess what?"

He looked around to see Sarah Cherone and Lexi Palmer rushing toward him. Sarah had curly blond hair and was kind of chubby. There were two things she liked. One was food—and the other was Fitz.

Sarah's best friend, Lexi, had straight brown hair, was thin, and wore glasses. Fitz didn't really know her very well. All he knew was that she was kind of a nerd. She had all kinds of allergies, and half her school lunch was always vitamins and pills.

"Hi, Fitz," Sarah said again. She batted her eyelashes at him the way she always did. It was disgusting. Then she and Lexi giggled.

"Hi," he mumbled, feeling grumpier than ever. The last thing he wanted to do on his birthday was get stuck talking to Sarah. That was even worse than having to go to school. Well, almost.

"You're never going to believe this," Lexi said breathlessly. "Tell him, Sarah."

"Yeah, Fitz. Our school has a new cook!"

Fitz frowned at her as if she'd lost her mind. "Big deal," he replied. "Who cares about a crummy cook?"

"You will when you see her," Lexi assured him. "This cook is seriously weird."

"Her name's Miss Larva Webb, and she's got—" Sarah went on, but Fitz tuned her out.

He couldn't stand to listen to her. She bugged him all the time. The year before, she had told his best friend, Brian Collins, that she liked Fitz. She was always passing him stupid notes in class. Sometimes they had hearts drawn on them. Stupid hearts with stupid arrows stuck through them. Fitz hated all girls, but he hated Sarah the most.

"Hey, Traflon. Over here."

Brian's voice cut into Fitz's thoughts. He spun around, breaking into a grin—his first smile of the day. Good old Brian. He'd save Fitz from the girls' ridiculous gossiping about the new cook.

"What's up?" Fitz called as he hurried toward Brian.

"Hey, happy birthday, man. I've got something to show you," Brian said excitedly. "Come on."

"What is it?" Fitz asked as he followed his best friend toward the school building.

4

"You'll see," said Brian.

"What's the big mystery?" Fitz asked. He wondered if Brian had some kind of surprise birthday present for him inside. Maybe this birthday wouldn't turn out to be a total loss. Fitz eagerly tried to figure out what the surprise could be. "Come on, tell me," he begged.

"No way. You've got to see it yourself to believe it," said Brian, pulling open the heavy front door and hurrying inside.

The moment Fitz realized they were heading toward the cafeteria, his heart sank with a thud. "This doesn't have anything to do with the new cook, does it?" he asked.

Brian nodded and grinned. "Just wait until you see her."

"Give me a break, Brian," Fitz said, his bad mood returning instantly. "What's the big deal about a stupid new cook?"

Brian pushed open the big double doors to the lunchroom and dragged him inside. Pulling Fitz down behind a table, Brian pointed toward a pudgy woman who was polishing the empty steam tables with a cloth. Her back was to them, but Fitz could hear her humming tunelessly as she worked.

Fitz rolled his eyes in exasperation. The cook was an older woman with curly white hair. A white apron was tied around her ample waist, and a tall chef's hat was perched on her head. She didn't look much different from any other school cook Fitz had ever seen—although when she turned her head a little, he noticed that she was wearing large dark sunglasses.

"She looks pretty normal to me, except for the glasses," Fitz whispered. "Maybe she's blind or something."

"She's not blind. But just wait until she turns around," Brian urged, his eyes glittering.

Fitz shrugged, rolled his eyes, and waited. Finally the woman turned to dip her rag into a bucket behind her, and Fitz did a double take.

The cook was wearing a weird-looking necklace. It was a chain with lots of little baubles hanging from it. And the baubles seemed to be moving!

Fitz frowned. "Am I seeing things?" he whispered, squinting at the necklace.

Brian shook his head. "No way."

Fitz raised his head to get a better look. His eyes widened, and he gasped in horror. The baubles on the cook's necklace were *bugs.*

And they were alive!

Chapter

"Let's get out of here," Fitz whispered to Brian under his breath.

Brian nodded. But at that moment the cook looked up and spotted them.

"Boys, I'm so glad you came by to say hello," she exclaimed happily.

She was smiling. She looked like somebody's grandmother, except for the sunglasses—and, of course, the wiggling bugs around her neck. The sight of the necklace made Fitz's skin crawl.

"Come over here, boys, and introduce yourselves," she ordered.

Fitz and Brian hesitated for a second. But then they did as they were told.

As they got closer to the cook, Fitz stared at her necklace. The bugs seemed to have stopped moving.

In fact, the more closely he inspected them, the more they looked like little plastic models.

How could I have thought they were alive? he wondered.

"I see you like my necklace," said the cook. "Pretty little things, aren't they?" She held it up so they could see. The bugs were made of plastic.

"You didn't think they were real, did you?" she asked Fitz, turning to look at him. Or at least Fitz assumed she was looking at him. With those huge dark glasses covering her eyes it was hard to tell. For a second Fitz had the eerie feeling that the huge, round black lenses *were* her eyes.

He suddenly realized he was staring openmouthed at the necklace. He shook his head, feeling a little dizzy.

The cook laughed out loud. "Oh, my! That's funny. Of course they're not real. They'd never allow me to bring bugs into the kitchen. Everyone knows bugs and food don't mix!" She laughed even harder at that.

Then, turning serious, she went on. "My name is Miss Larva Webb. But you boys can call me Miss Larva. I hope we can become great friends."

Fitz was still staring at the necklace. He couldn't tear his gaze away from it. He saw that there was a long-legged praying mantis near the center and a couple of fat grasshoppers on either side. There were wasps, termites, and a dragonfly up one side of the chain, and a few beetles, a moth, and a giant water bug on the other side. Fitz had never seen anything like it.

Suddenly he felt Brian nudge him.

He shot a quick look at his friend, who nodded toward the cook's smiling face.

"Young man, weren't you listening? I said, I hope we can be great friends."

Fitz gulped nervously and tried once again to see her eyes through the dark lenses of her sunglasses.

"Uh, yeah, um, me too. N-nice to meet you, Miss Larva," he stammered.

"My name is Brian Collins," Brian told the cook politely. "He's Fitz Traflon."

"I see you're still admiring my necklace, Fitz. I'm very flattered. You see, I made it myself. Isn't it lovely?" Miss Larva said proudly. "I'm an amateur entomologist—a bug person. I've been studying insects from the time I could crawl. I've learned some fascinating things in that time." She touched the necklace lovingly. "Including how to make friends with all the dear little bugs. This necklace reminds me of them when we can't be together." Her voice was almost a purr.

Fitz backed slowly toward the door. "Um, your necklace is really nice. We'd better get going now," he said. He knew his voice was shaking. "Nice to meet you, Miss Bug—er, Miss Larva."

"Yeah, nice to meet you," echoed Brian.

The boys exchanged looks of relief as they headed for the cafeteria door.

Suddenly something darted across the floor in front of Fitz.

"Yuck! A cockroach!" he cried. Racing after it, he smashed his foot down on top of it and heard a soft squishing sound. "I hate cockroaches," he mumbled with a shudder as he stood over the oozing, flattened bug and watched it flail its tiny legs jerkily in the air.

"What have you done?" shrieked Miss Larva. She rushed over to the squished cockroach and dropped to her hands and knees. "That's Gregory! He's one of my pets!"

Fitz watched in disbelief as the cook prodded the roach with the tip of her fingernail. The sight made him want to vomit.

"Gregory? Gregory, my sweet?" Miss Larva cooed softly. "It's Mommy. Give me a sign that you're alive, my baby."

The cockroach slowly kicked two of its legs. Once. Twice. And then the legs stopped, frozen in midair.

"Gregory?" Miss Larva cried. "Don't die. You can't die. *Please* don't die!"

She gently poked at the insect again, but there

was no response. His legs were still.

She gently picked up Gregory and laid him inside one cupped hand. Then, with tears streaming down her face, she slowly got to her feet and carried him over to the lunchroom counter. She pulled a paper napkin out of a holder and folded it into a small square. Tenderly she put Gregory down on the napkin and gave a soft sigh of resignation.

Then, her face smoldering with rage, she whirled to face Fitz. As she did, her dark glasses slipped down her nose.

"Murderer," she hissed.

Fitz stared at her, unable to speak. Her eyes, clearly visible for the first time, were burning into his.

He stepped back, his heart pounding. Miss Larva's eyes were different from any human eyes he had ever seen. He wanted to look away, but he couldn't. He stared into them, seeing that each of her unusually large pupils was made up of hundreds of tiny little eyes, each looking in a slightly different direction.

Where had he seen eyes like that before? Then he remembered—he'd seen them in a close-up photograph in his science book last year. *Miss Larva's eyes looked just like the eyes of a fly.*

Chapter

"Didn't I say you'd have to see her to believe her?" Brian asked as soon as the boys were out in the hall again.

"Yeah," replied Fitz. "She's really weird. Did you see her eyes?"

Brian shook his head. "Nah, I was too busy looking at the bugs on her necklace. I almost thought they were alive when I first saw them. But even though they're only plastic, it's still pretty wild! Can you imagine any other adult wearing something like that?"

Fitz opened his mouth to tell Brian about the cook's eyes and then stopped himself. Now that he was away from the cafeteria, it didn't seem real. Maybe he'd just imagined that her eyes looked like the eyes of a fly. After all, he was still pretty shaken up by his two roach encounters that day. He decided to do his best to forget all about Miss Larva Webb.

That morning Fitz had a hard time concentrating on school. For one thing his teacher, Mrs. Dewberry, assigned Sarah Cherone the seat directly in front of him. As she flounced over to her seat and flashed him a grin, Fitz sighed. It was going to be a long year.

It was bad enough that Sarah couldn't sit still and that her wiggling caused strands of her short, curly blond hair to bounce in front of his eyes like springs. But to make it worse, she was constantly looking over her shoulder and batting her eyes at him.

Once when the teacher's back was turned, Sarah spun around and gave him a toothy grin. "Have you seen the new cook yet, Fitz?"

Fitz heaved a bored sigh and looked at the ceiling. He didn't answer. Finally she took the hint and turned around again.

He was glad. But Sarah's comment started him thinking about Miss Larva. He shook his head as he remembered how he had almost called her Miss Buggy to her face. Still, it would have been a better name for her.

What kind of weirdo wears bugs on her necklace and keeps a cockroach named Gregory for a pet? he wondered. *And those eyes!* He couldn't stop the shudder that ran through him when he thought of her buggy fly eyes—even though by now he had almost convinced himself that he'd imagined the whole thing.

The morning seemed to drag on forever. English

14

was boring. Math was boring. But in the middle of social studies, Fitz began to notice an appetizing smell drifting into the classroom. He sniffed the air curiously.

Is it my imagination, he wondered, *or do I smell pizza?*

He looked at the clock above Mrs. Dewberry's desk. It was almost time for lunch.

Fitz took a deep breath, inhaling the delicious aroma. It was definitely pizza. But it didn't smell like the crummy pizza the cafeteria usually served. The crust on that pizza had been tougher than cardboard, and the cheese had tasted like plastic. That pizza had been one of the reasons Fitz had started bringing his lunch from home.

But this pizza smelled delicious.

Closing his eyes, Fitz began daydreaming about thick, tangy tomato sauce and spicy pepperoni. This was more like it—the perfect birthday lunch. He couldn't believe his luck. His stomach was roaring by the time the lunch bell rang.

He had bolted out of his seat and pushed his way to the door before he remembered he had brought his lunch. Sighing, he went back to his desk and pulled out his smushed and soggy sandwich and walked to the lunchroom. The closer he got to the cafeteria, the better the pizza smelled.

"Some birthday lunch," he grumbled. He wished he had enough money to buy a slice of pizza, but his pockets were empty.

"Smells good, huh?" Brian asked sadly when he and Fitz found a table.

Fitz nodded and gazed longingly toward some kids at the next table who were eating pizza. "Get a load of that," he said. "Look how big and thick those slices are."

"Yeah," Brian agreed, nibbling halfheartedly on his bologna sandwich. "And there's so much cheese on them that it strings out as far as their arms can reach."

"Yeah," said Fitz enviously.

"I'll tell you one thing, if Miss Larva is this good a cook, I'm not bringing my lunch tomorrow." Brian pitched his sandwich onto the table in disgust. "Are you?"

"I dunno," muttered Fitz. He couldn't help remembering how much Miss Larva liked bugs and how much he hated them. And he also remembered how she had yelled at him for stepping on her pet cockroach.

I'm not sure I could eat anything Miss Buggy cooked, no matter how good it looked, he thought.

Just then the kitchen door swung open, and Miss Larva came marching out. There was a big smile on her face, and her chef's hat sat high on her head. She was carrying a huge three-tiered cake on a gigantic platter in front of her. The cake looked fantastic. It was over four feet high, and every layer was slathered with thick white frosting.

To Fitz's amazement Miss Larva marched straight over to where he was sitting and set the cake squarely in front of him. His mouth dropped open.

Written on the cake in fancy letters were the words:

HAPPY BIRTHDAY,
FITZGERALD TRAFLON III

Fitz looked at the cake, then at the cook, and then back at the cake again. Miss Larva was beaming at him expectantly.

"Brian, did you tell her it's my birthday?" he demanded in a whisper.

"No way," Brian insisted. "You'd have heard me if I had, dude."

By that time the other kids in the cafeteria had spotted the cake and were gathering around the boys' table.

"Hey, Fitz," shouted Jeff McCormick. "How about a piece?"

"Yeah, Fitz. I hope you're going to share," said Sarah, gazing hungrily at the towering cake from the next table, where she was sitting with Lexi.

"Of course he's going to share," said Miss Larva. She produced paper dessert plates and extra forks from the large pockets of her apron and began cutting the cake into pieces.

Mrs. Dewberry stood up at her table and clapped her hands. "Let's all sing 'Happy Birthday' to Fitz," she suggested with a smile.

Fitz looked around in amazement as the en-

17

tire lunchroom began singing to him.

Maybe this isn't going to be such a bad birthday after all, he thought.

When the song was finished, Miss Larva held up her hand for silence. "The birthday boy gets the first bite," she announced loudly.

There were a few groans from the crowd, but most kids held up their forks to signal that they were waiting.

"Go ahead," urged Sarah.

"Yeah, hurry up so we can eat ours," said Brian. "It looks awesome."

The cake looked so delicious, his mouth was watering. Fitz pushed all the doubts he'd had about Miss Larva to the back of his mind. He scooped up a bite of cake on his fork. "Hey, look. It's got chocolate chips in it," he cried, popping the cake into his mouth and swallowing it.

"Oh, no, those aren't chocolate chips," said Miss Larva, shaking her head. "They're much better for you than chocolate chips." A grin spread across her pudgy face. "They're chocolate-covered ants!"

"Ha-ha," said Jeff McCormick, rolling his eyes as he wolfed down his slice of cake. "Good one, Miss Larva!" The rest of the kids started laughing, too.

All except for Fitz. He was too busy gagging.

Chapter

Fitz stuck his finger down his throat and retched. But nothing came up. He thought about dozens of chocolate-covered ants swimming around in his stomach. He retched harder.

Lexi was giving him a disgusted look from the next table. Fitz noticed that she hadn't touched her slice of cake. He figured she must be allergic to it, like she was to just about everything else.

Fitz was about to stick two fingers down his throat when Miss Larva climbed onto a chair and held up her hands for silence.

"Children, listen to me!" she shouted. "I want you to know that ants are dear little creatures while they're alive. But once they die, and their little bodies are dipped in chocolate, they make wonderful food. And so do many of our other little six-legged friends—fried grasshoppers, for instance. Why, in many parts of the world they're considered a delicacy."

Fitz stopped trying to throw up and listened. Everyone else was listening, too. He noticed some of the teachers exchanging smiles. The principal, Mr. Gladstone, winked at Mrs. Dewberry and chuckled.

"And best of all," Miss Larva went on, stabbing the air with a finger for emphasis. "Best of all, boys and girls, they are *protein,* the building blocks of the body. They are very nutritious. Now, isn't that wonderful?"

"Thank you, Miss Larva, for that very interesting bit of information," said Mr. Gladstone with a grin. By this time most of the kids and teachers were laughing. Some of them applauded when Miss Larva gave a little bow and headed back toward the kitchen.

Fitz stared down at the cake on his plate. Had Miss Larva really been kidding about the chocolate-covered ants? Most of his classmates seemed to think so. Many of them had already returned for second or even third helpings of the cake. Fitz had to admit that the one bite he had taken had tasted pretty good. Actually, it had tasted terrific. He picked up his fork, and he finished his cake in three more bites. But he secretly picked out the chocolate chips and hid them in his napkin—just in case.

The next day a lot of kids who normally brought their lunches from home were in the line to buy lunch, including Brian.

Fitz had thought about it that morning, but he still didn't quite trust Miss Larva. Once again he brought a peanut-butter-and-jelly sandwich from home. He didn't want to eat anything else the new cook made until he knew more about what she was putting into the food.

He clutched his sandwich and watched as Miss Larva filled other students' plates with big juicy cheeseburgers and french fries. Fitz's mouth watered furiously.

"Not a bad-looking burger," he said, looking at Brian's plate. "But I'd rather have my lunch."

"Uh-huh," said Brian, giving Fitz a skeptical look. "Sure you would."

Fitz grinned slyly. "Didn't you hear that Miss Buggy's french fries are really fried grasshoppers?"

"Cool," said Brian, popping one of his fries into his mouth and chewing noisily. "Grasshoppers are the building blocks of the body, you know." He grinned, revealing the partially chewed contents of his mouth. Fitz's stomach gave a shudder. Was it his imagination, or did the chewed-up french fry look a little green?

"Forget it," Fitz said, looking away.

But Brian wasn't through. "See, what Miss Larva

does," he said, "is she grinds up the grasshoppers in this big meat grinder. Then when she's got this big mushy mess, she shapes it to look like french fries and cooks them. Yum yum." He popped another one into his mouth.

Fitz made a face. "Yeah, well, I wouldn't put it past Miss Buggy," he muttered, staring down at his sandwich.

Brian stared straight at Fitz for a moment and frowned. "You're just jealous, man. It's nobody's fault but your own that you're missing out on this great food. Now, quit calling her Miss Buggy and pass the mustard."

Fitz looked around for the mustard, but there wasn't any on the table. "You'll have to borrow from another table," he said.

Brian picked up another long, golden french fry and stuffed it into his mouth. Fitz watched Brian chew his french fry. He looked at Brian's burger. The smell was driving him crazy.

"How'd Miss Bug-Larva know my full name was Fitzgerald Traflon the Third?" asked Fitz. "Did you tell her?"

"How could I have?" said Brian. "I told you, you were with me in the kitchen, remember? Now, come on, where's the mustard? I need it for my burger."

Usually there was salt, pepper, mustard, and ketchup on each lunch table. Fitz glanced around at the other tables. There was salt, pepper, and ketchup on all of them, but no mustard.

"I guess you'll have to go ask for some," said Fitz with a shrug.

Brian got up and hurried over to the cook, who was still standing behind the steam table. Fitz was left alone at the table.

Maybe I could steal one french fry, thought Fitz. *Brian would never know.*

Fitz's hand was inching across the table toward the biggest fry on the plate when he heard Miss Larva let out a roar.

"MUSTARD! How dare you ask for mustard?" she shouted. Her face was beet-red, and her hands were clenched into fists. "I never allow mustard in my cafeteria. It's *terrible* on food! Now, go eat your lunch!"

Fitz pulled his hand away just in time as Brian raced back to the table.

"Did you see that?" Brian asked in astonishment, glancing back at the cook. "What tripped her trigger? All I did was ask for mustard."

"Who knows?" said Fitz with a shrug. "Maybe she's having a bad hair day or something." He stared at Brian's french fries. Even without mustard he'd rather have Brian's lunch than his own. His peanut-butter sandwich was sticking to the roof of his mouth like concrete.

Maybe tomorrow, he thought hungrily.

Chapter

The next morning Lexi stopped Fitz as he was coming onto the playground.

"Can I talk to you for a minute?" she asked.

Fitz rolled his eyes. He had enough problems. He had decided to bring his lunch from home again today, and now he was regretting it. He was already in a bad mood, and talking to a girl wasn't likely to help.

"What do you want?" mumbled Fitz. He realized he'd never really talked to Lexi before unless Sarah was there, too.

"You aren't going to buy your lunch today, are you?" Lexi asked urgently.

Fitz frowned. "What's it to you?"

"I was just wondering," said Lexi, looking a little hurt.

Fitz instantly felt guilty for snapping at her. He wished she would go away and leave him alone, but she just stood there staring at him.

Finally he sighed and said, "No, I brought my lunch."

"I'm glad," said Lexi, looking relieved.

"Why do you care?" Fitz asked, a little curious in spite of himself.

Lexi held out her hand. In it were four dark-red specks. They looked like dead ants.

"What's that?" asked Fitz, leaning forward for a closer look.

"They're insects. They belong to the genus . . ."

"Whoa, you're as bad as Miss Buggy!" said Fitz, backing away from her. "They're ants!" *Why does she have to be such a nerd?* he wondered. "Don't give them to me. I don't want them."

"I wasn't going to give them to you. I just wanted you to see them," she replied irritably.

"So I see them. So what?"

"I took some of the chocolate chips from the birth-day cake Miss Larva made you the other day," she explained. "These were in them. She wasn't kidding."

Fitz did a double take. He stared at the dead ant bodies in Lexi's hand. "No way," he said.

"Way," she replied, looking smug. "I just thought you should know. I don't know about you, but *I'm* certainly not going to eat any of Miss Bug—er . . . Miss Larva's cooking."

Fitz looked at her in disbelief. Was Lexi making this up? Or had there really been ants in the cake? Things were getting weirder and weirder. He mumbled something about having to get to homeroom and hurried away. When he glanced back over his shoulder, though, Lexi was still staring after him.

At lunch that day Fitz watched as the students and teachers crowded into line. Miss Larva was behind the steam table as usual, serving up heaping portions of tacos, refried beans, and rice.

When Brian came out of the lunch line, he hurried over to the table and sat down across from Fitz. He immediately started digging into his food without even saying hello.

Fitz looked nervously at the food on Brian's plate. Were the little lumps in the beans really beans—or were they some kind of beetle? And the rice. Were all those little white grains really rice—or could they be maggots?

Fitz tried to put those crazy thoughts out of his mind. Brian's plate wasn't full of beetles and maggots. It was full of beans and rice. Still, Fitz had seen maggots once when he had forgotten to empty a can of fishing worms for a couple of weeks in the summertime. And that was exactly what they had looked like—a can full of squirming grains of rice.

While Brian wolfed down his food, Fitz munched halfheartedly on his sandwich and cautiously looked around. Ordinarily the room was filled with the sounds of kids talking and laughing as they ate. But at that moment all the kids had their heads down and were shoveling food into their mouths in silence. Even the teachers were stuffing tacos into their mouths as fast as they could.

He scanned the room for Lexi. She was sitting at a table with Sarah, and she was watching the others eat, too. She noticed Fitz looking at her and she shrugged. Then she popped one of her allergy pills into her mouth.

Miss Larva was standing behind the steam table, beaming benevolently at the students and teachers. She sighed and absently removed her sunglasses to wipe them off.

Suddenly she saw Fitz looking at her. Her smile froze as she stared back at him.

Even from that distance he could see the hundreds of tiny irises of her fly's eyes glaring at him. Her eyes seemed to have grown larger since the first time he'd seen them. He wanted to look away, but he couldn't. His gaze was fixed on those eyes.

A moment later a sudden motion across the room finally dragged Fitz's attention away. It was Lexi. She was standing up, her face a ghostly white. Instantly Fitz understood. Lexi was staring at Miss Larva's eyes, and there was a look of terror on her face.

Chapter

fter lunch Fitz followed Brian to the tray-return window.

Before he put the tray through the window, Brian licked the remaining beans off his plate. He grinned at Fitz. "Awesome," he said. "You really ought to try Miss Larva's cooking, Fitz. You don't know what you're missing."

As they headed for the exit, Fitz spotted a hand-printed sign tacked to the bulletin board just inside the door. "Hey, Brian. Check it out," he said. The boys stopped to read the sign.

ATTENTION ALL STUDENTS
COME TO THE CAFETERIA AFTER SCHOOL TODAY
AND LEARN ALL ABOUT SOME NEW AND
WONDERFUL CREATURES. YOU'LL BE AMAZED!

"Wow, what do you think that's all about?" Brian asked excitedly.

Fitz shrugged. "I dunno," he said. He was still thinking more about Lexi and Miss Larva's weird eyes than about the sign.

"Are you going?" asked Brian.

"No, I've got better things to do after school," Fitz replied. "Are you?"

"Sure. I wouldn't miss it for anything," Brian said. "I can't believe you don't want to go."

The bell rang before Fitz could answer. All through his afternoon classes Fitz couldn't stop thinking about Miss Larva. Now that Lexi had seen her eyes, too, Fitz knew that they had to be real. He wondered whether he should tell his parents or Mr. Gladstone. But he decided that if he tried to tell them the new school cook had eyes like a fly, they would just think he was crazy. He had to find out more about Miss Larva first. And the best way to do that, he realized, was to go to the meeting in the cafeteria after school.

As soon as the final bell rang, Fitz hurried to the cafeteria. There he spotted Brian at a long table near the front.

Brian looked surprised for a second and then gestured for Fitz to join him. There was only one empty seat left at the table, and Fitz squeezed through the crowd and dropped into it.

"Thought you weren't coming," said Brian. He grinned slyly. "I guess you just couldn't resist Miss Larva's charm, could you?"

"Chill out, okay?" Fitz retorted. He looked around the room. It looked as though every student in the whole school was there.

Suddenly the doors to the kitchen swung open and Miss Larva came bumping into the room, her arms loaded with small wire cages. Each cage was covered with cloth, hiding what was inside.

Brian leaned closer to Fitz. "What do you think she's got in those cages? Something weird?"

Fitz shook his head. "Couldn't be any weirder than she is," he muttered.

Miss Larva set the cages in a row on a table. Then she bent over each of them, cooing softly as if she were talking to the creatures inside.

Fitz squirmed uneasily in his seat and glanced to his right. Lexi was sitting across the aisle next to Sarah. She was staring at Miss Larva's cages.

"Maybe Miss Buggy's got Gregory's brothers and sisters in those cages," Fitz whispered to Brian. "What if she turns them loose and lets them crawl all over everybody?" Fitz had meant it to be a

31

joke, but he was embarrassed to hear that his voice was shaking.

Luckily, Brian didn't seem to notice. "Cool," he whispered back with a grin, his eyes fixed on the cages.

"She probably has them all named, like Timothy and Robert and Jordan, and she'll throw a fit if anyone says something mean about one of her babies," Fitz went on, more to himself than to Brian. He shuddered.

"Check it out," whispered Brian. Miss Larva was holding up her hands for attention. Instantly all eyes were on her.

Fitz looked her over closely. She was wearing her sunglasses as usual, and the plastic bugs on her necklace swung around as she moved her arms.

"Thank you for coming, boys and girls," Miss Larva began. "As many of you already know, I'm an amateur entomologist—a bug person."

Laughter rippled through the crowd.

"I study insects," she went on. "I also study spiders. I hope this program and many more like it will inspire some of you to become interested in my fascinating hobby."

Murmurs raced through the room like wildfire.

"Ugh."

"No way!"

"Get serious."

Miss Larva smiled patiently. When everybody was quiet again, she continued. "Many people fear insects needlessly. Actually, most are quite harmless. The dear little creatures are fun to watch and easy to get acquainted with. Why, I'll bet there are some of you who've had ant farms, so you know that already."

"No way," mumbled Fitz to himself. He would never have an ant farm.

"But most of all, they are fun to experiment with," the cook said. She paused for a moment to let this statement sink in. "Yes, that's what I said. They're fun to experiment with, and I'm going to show you the results of some of my finest experiments."

Fitz exchanged nervous glances with Brian. Neither boy could imagine what was coming next.

The cook picked up one of the cages, but didn't remove the cloth cover. "My greatest joy is crossbreeding. That means I take one kind of insect and breed it with another kind to see what kind of amazing and fascinating creature I will get. For instance . . ." She held the cage high so everyone could see, and pulled off the cover with a flourish.

Fitz gasped. "Whoa, Brian, look at that thing!"

". . . I crossed a tarantula and a centipede, and look what I got," said Miss Larva proudly.

She reached into the cage and pulled out a huge

wiggling insect. Its body was long and narrow like a centipede's, and it had at least a hundred legs. But those legs were long and extremely hairy. The insect was black all over and stood more than two inches tall.

"Cool," said Brian, leaning forward for a better look. "Hey, Fitz. Check it out."

But Sarah had quite a different reaction. She let out a bloodcurdling scream and clutched at Lexi's arm. "Oh, yuck!" she shrieked. A few other kids squirmed and giggled nervously.

For once Fitz had to agree with Sarah. "Gross," he whispered to himself.

Brian's hand shot into the air. "Miss Larva, how do you do a thing like that?"

"That's my secret," she replied with a mysterious smile.

Next she brought out a creature with six long thin legs and graceful red, gray, and white wings. "This, boys and girls, is a cross between a spider and a butterfly." She opened yet another cage. "And here is a combination wasp and grasshopper." The angrily buzzing insect hopped across the table, making Fitz jump with alarm.

As quickly as she had brought them out, Miss Larva whisked the creatures back into their cages and covered them with cloth again.

When that was finished, she took a deep breath.

"And now, children, for some really exciting news."

Fitz stared at her, watching her face take on a strange glow.

When she spoke again, her voice vibrated just above a whisper. "Very soon you will all help me with the greatest experiment I've ever conducted. I can't tell you about it now, but very soon you'll understand."

All the kids started whispering excitedly. All except Fitz. He shivered at her words. Miss Larva's mouth was turned up in a big smile. And the bugs on her necklace seemed to move just a little bit.

Chapter

"Hey, did you hear that?" Brian asked excitedly as the two boys headed for home a few minutes later. "Miss Larva said we're going to be part of her greatest experiment ever. Doesn't that sound cool?"

"I guess so," Fitz answered nervously. But deep down inside he wasn't so sure.

"I hope she'll let me cross a scorpion with something," said Brian. "They're wild. Maybe I'll cross a scorpion with a—"

"Listen, Brian, I need to talk to you about Miss Buggy," Fitz broke in. "She's . . . well, she's spooky. She might even be dangerous. Have you ever noticed her eyes?"

"What about her eyes?" snapped Brian. "Who can see them behind those sunglasses she's always wearing? And I told you to quit calling her Miss Buggy."

"Okay, okay. So you've never seen her eyes. Believe me, Brian, they're not the least bit normal."

Brian gave him a skeptical look. "What are you talking about?"

Fitz took a deep breath. He knew it was going to be hard to explain. "The pupils, they're . . . well, the pupils are like . . . like a fly's eye. They're made up of all these little eyes. Honest. If you look real close, you'll see it for yourself."

Brian threw back his head and roared with laughter. "Traflon, you're a nutcase! *Eyes like a fly?* That's a good one. How'd you think that up?"

"I didn't think it up," Fitz replied angrily. "You don't have to believe me. Go see for yourself."

"Sure, I'll just go ask her to take off her sunglasses so I can check out her fly eyes," Brian said sarcastically. He chuckled again. "You're really losing it, dude. In the meantime don't bad-mouth Miss Larva, okay? She's cool, and her cooking is even better than my mom's. Her burgers and fries are out of this world, even without mustard. As a matter of fact, I've decided that hers are the only ones I'm going to eat from now on."

Fitz didn't answer. There was no use talking to Brian. He was obviously too carried away with Miss Larva's weird experiments—not to mention her cooking—to listen to reason.

The next morning at school Fitz tried to talk to some of his other friends about Miss Larva, but none of them would listen either. Every time he brought up her name, kids would start praising her cooking.

"Man, you've got a lot of nerve putting Miss Larva down," said Jeff McCormick. "Especially after she made you that incredible birthday cake. Just because you're too stupid to buy your lunch, don't try to ruin it for the rest of us."

"You ought to have your head examined," said Eric Plummer when Fitz approached him. "Miss Larva's food is the best we've ever had in this cafeteria. Would you rather have that terrible cook we had last year come back?"

In desperation Fitz decided to talk to Lexi about it. He hurried outside and spotted her on the playground.

"Hey, Lexi," he said, running up to her. "I need to talk to you about Miss Buggy."

"Hello, Fitz," said a familiar sickly sweet voice. Too late Fitz noticed that Sarah was with Lexi. He groaned in dismay, but Sarah didn't notice. She was fluttering her eyelashes at him. "Why do you call her Miss Buggy, Fitz? That's not a very nice name," she said with a flirtatious pout.

Fitz clenched his fists at his sides and glanced at

Lexi in desperation. She was gazing at him thoughtfully, but she didn't say anything. Fitz turned back to Sarah, feeling annoyed that Lexi obviously wasn't going to help him out. "I call her that because Miss Buggy is part fly," he said in his nastiest voice. He held his arms out like wings and made a buzzing sound.

Sarah wrinkled her nose. "Oh, *gross*! Don't say things like that."

"Well, she is," Fitz insisted. "Just get her to take off her sunglasses and look at her eyes. They've got all these little bitty eyes inside them, and they can look all different directions at once. I'll bet she eats slimy rotten stuff out of the garbage can." He paused. "I saw some rotten wormy tomatoes out in the Dumpster this morning—maybe she'll make sandwiches out of it and serve it for lunch!"

Sarah turned green and her mouth started to quiver.

"It's true," Fitz insisted, backing away from her. "I hope you like tomato mush, Sarah. But watch out for the worms—they can be crunchy."

Just then Sarah grabbed her stomach and opened her mouth. Then she heaved and threw up all over her shoes.

Lexi shot Fitz a dirty look. "What did you have to do that for?" she hissed as she hurried to help her friend. "We're going to have enough trouble getting people to believe us about Miss Buggy as it is!" She put her arm around Sarah's shoulders and led her off in the direction of the girls' bathroom.

Fitz shoved his hands into his pockets and wandered away in the opposite direction. He was glad that somebody finally believed him, even if it was only Lexi. But now he wished he hadn't goofed around and made Sarah throw up—maybe he could have gotten Lexi alone and talked to her about what to do.

By the second week of school Fitz and Lexi were the only ones still bringing their lunch. In fact, most of the other kids were even complaining about having to stay home on weekends and eat their parents' cooking—despite the fact that Miss Larva's menus had gotten a little strange. Although she usually served normal things like spaghetti or hot dogs, she had started occasionally fixing more bizarre meals as well. One day she served eggplant-and-zucchini casserole with a side dish of deep-fried frogs' legs. Another time she presented the students with a deep-dish sardine pizza with pineapple chunks. Both times Fitz had been disgusted by the sight of the food, but had secretly thought it smelled pretty good.

That wasn't the only thing that was different around school these days, though. Fitz had noticed that the teachers were getting nicer and nicer—even the ones who were really strict or mean. All of a sudden none of them were giving homework anymore. Tests were unbelievably easy. For the first time in his life Fitz was getting A's and B's.

But perhaps the strangest change of all was in everyone's appetites. They were getting bigger and bigger with every passing day. Especially Brian's.

"Look at all the food on your plate," Fitz said one day when Brian came to the table with four pieces of fried chicken, two helpings of mashed potatoes and gravy, and five warm buttered rolls. "You can't possibly eat all that."

Brian stuffed a roll into his mouth. "Uh course ah can," he said.

Fitz nibbled on a bologna sandwich and watched Brian devour everything on his plate and go back for a second helping. This time Brian had six rolls and five pieces of chicken, and they were sitting on top of an entire plateful of mashed potatoes and gravy.

It almost made Fitz sick to his stomach to see all that food. But Brian ate every bite. He even sopped up the last of the gravy with a roll. Then he looked sadly at his empty plate.

"How can you eat so much?" Fitz asked as he followed Brian to the tray return.

"I keep telling you, dude, it's Miss Larva's cooking," Brian said with a burp. "It's great!"

Fitz nodded, but he didn't say anything. At least the food had looked pretty normal lately. There had been nothing to remind him of beetles or maggots.

"You don't know what you're missing," Brian went on.

"That's right," said Sarah. She and Lexi had just come up behind them. "It shows how stupid you are." Sarah was eating a gigantic brownie. It was that day's dessert, and it looked delicious. It looked moist and chewy, and it was packed with nuts. Fitz could hardly take his eyes off it. He heard his stomach grumble.

"What about Lexi?" asked Fitz, tearing his eyes away from the brownie with difficulty. "I haven't seen her eat any of Miss Larva's food either."

"Lexi's different," said Sarah with a shrug, glancing at her friend. "She has to bring her lunch because of her allergies. But you don't. And you bad-mouth Miss Larva and call her names when you don't even know how great her food is. Just looking at you makes me want to throw up again!" With that Sarah spun around and pranced away.

"Sarah's right. You're just being stubborn," said Brian. "I don't know what the big deal is. You've got to be a moron to want your puny little sandwiches instead of Miss Larva's great food."

Fitz threw up his arms in frustration. Why was he the only kid in school who didn't trust Miss Larva?

Maybe he really was overreacting. Just because she had eyes like a fly didn't mean she was out to poison the whole school or anything. Besides, he was really getting curious about her famous cooking. That brownie sure had looked delicious—not to mention the fried chicken and mashed potatoes. Maybe he should try buying his lunch, just once. Just to find out what the big deal was. How much harm could it do?

"Okay, okay!" said Fitz, almost before he knew what he was saying. "I'll do it tomorrow. I'll buy my lunch."

Chapter

Fitz headed for school earlier than usual the next morning. He had lunch money in his pocket instead of a sandwich in his backpack. He wasn't going to go back on his promise to Brian.

But he wasn't going to eat Miss Larva's cooking without finding out a few things, either.

When he got to school, the playground was empty. He slipped in the front door and looked around. The halls were deserted. He could see teachers in their classrooms, preparing for the day. Luckily none of them noticed him as he tiptoed down the hall.

Fitz's heart fluttered in his chest as he stopped in front of the double doors to the cafeteria. *What if she catches me?* he wondered nervously. *She might grind me up and turn me into meat loaf!*

The idea made him shudder. Taking a deep breath,

he pushed open the door and slipped inside the deserted lunchroom. Silently he moved among the empty tables toward the kitchen door. As he got closer, he heard singing coming from inside the kitchen.

"Itsy-bitsy spider, climbed up the waterspout."

Fitz's eyes widened. It was Miss Larva. She was singing to herself.

He swallowed hard and eased the door open a couple of inches, being careful not to make a sound. By closing one eye and looking through the crack with the other, he could see the cook.

She had her back to him, and her chef's hat was perched on her head as usual. She was stirring something in a gigantic pan that covered the entire top of the stove.

Lunch! he thought, and gulped.

"Come in, Fitzgerald!" Miss Larva said suddenly in a commanding voice, without turning. "It's impolite to spy."

Fitz's other eye flew open. His heart started to pound, and his mouth went dry.

Her back is to me. How could she know I'm here? he thought frantically.

Miss Larva put her spoon down and slowly turned around. Staring straight at him, she boomed, "I said come in, Fitzgerald. *Now!*"

Opening the door wide, he went inside on shaking legs.

Chapter

Fitz wondered if Miss Larva could see how hard he was trembling.

She raised an eyebrow and studied him for a long time. Then she took off her sunglasses and studied him even harder.

To his alarm Fitz could see that the dark parts of her eyes had grown larger since the first time he'd seen them. The whites were now nothing more than a thin rim around the huge pupils.

"Why *were* you spying on me?" she demanded.

Fitz could hear a faint buzzing in the room. He trembled harder and tried to speak.

"I . . . I was . . . I mean . . ."

"*Fitzgerald,* answer my question!"

"I . . . I was just wondering what was for lunch," he said weakly.

A slow smile spread across Miss Larva's face. Her black eyes brightened. "Oh, I see! So you're enjoying my lunches, are you?" She sounded pleased.

The cook stepped aside and waved her hand toward the huge flat pan she had been stirring. It was the largest pan Fitz had ever seen.

He moved cautiously forward to take a closer look. In the pan was a thin layer of reddish sauce with lots of lumpy things swimming around in it.

He gasped and shrank back. "Those are *caterpillars*!" he cried in shock.

He couldn't take his eyes off the slimy writhing mass of caterpillars that filled the pan. Some of their thick pulsating bodies were green. Some were purple. Others were yellow or black-and-white-striped. Red gooey stuff clung to the fuzz on their bodies. He watched in horror as they crawled and squirmed over and around and under each other in the liquid. His stomach started doing flip-flops.

Miss Larva threw back her head and laughed heartily. She reached into the pan and picked up a large purple caterpillar with two fingers. Holding its dripping body high, she danced toward Fitz and stuck the squirming creature in front of his nose.

Fitz flinched and tried to move away, but the cook grabbed his arm with her free hand and held him tightly.

"Many insects go through four different stages to become adults," she said cheerfully. "The egg stage is the first one. The larva or caterpillar stage comes next. This is a larva—stage two."

Larva? thought Fitz. *That's Miss Buggy's name!*

Fitz stared in horror at the wriggling purple caterpillar. It was the ugliest thing he had ever seen.

A second later the cook whisked the larva away from his face and dropped it back into the pan.

Fitz curled his lip and wrinkled his nose in disgust as he watched it burrow into the moving mass of caterpillars.

While he was staring into the pan, Miss Larva produced a large jar of blood-red sauce. She opened the jar and began pouring the sauce over the larvae. Next she topped that with large slices of cheese. With each addition Fitz's mouth dropped open wider.

"Lasagna!" She announced cheerfully. Opening the oven door, she took the big pan off the stove and popped it inside. "Does that answer your question, Fitzgerald? We're having lasagna for lunch. My special recipe."

Fitz whirled around and crashed through the kitchen door. He was panting loudly as he streaked through the deserted lunchroom, knocking over chairs and bumping into tables.

Finally he reached the hallway. He ran all the way

to the main lobby, where he stopped and leaned against the wall. Perspiration was running down his face. Everything was silent except for the sound of his ragged breathing.

A second later the front doors burst open with a bang, and kids started pouring into the school, chattering and laughing. Fitz watched them as they headed for their lockers.

He was the only one who really knew what they were going to have for lunch.

And no one would believe him if he told them.

Chapter

As soon as he caught his breath, Fitz hurried outside to the playground. He searched frantically until he spotted Brian standing by the monkey bars.

"Brian!" he called, racing toward him.

Brian looked around and grinned. "What's the big rush? Your shoes on fire?"

"Listen, Brian. This is important," Fitz said as he skidded to a stop. "You're not going to believe this, but it's true. I swear it is."

"What are you talking about?" asked Brian.

"Miss Buggy, er, Miss Larva is cooking caterpillars for lunch," said Fitz. "I saw it with my own eyes."

Brian's expression changed—first to bewilderment, then to annoyance. He studied Fitz, frowning.

51

"You're a nut, Traflon. Did you know that? A real nut."

Fitz grabbed Brian's arm. "No, I'm not," he pleaded desperately. "Honest, Brian, I saw her do it. They were in this big pan, and they were wiggling around and everything. First she poured tomato sauce over them. Then she put cheese on top of that and put the pan in the oven. And then do you know what she said?"

Brian rolled his eyes and shook his head.

"She said, 'We're having lasagna for lunch.' That's what she said. I swear it," Fitz said. "You've got to believe me, Brian."

Brian shook his head again. "Hey, guys," he yelled to Jeff, Eric, and some other boys who were hanging out near the basketball court. "Fitz says Miss Larva's cooking lasagna with caterpillars in it for our lunch. Can you believe that?"

The boys went into fits of laughter as Fitz stared at Brian in disbelief. He couldn't believe his best friend was making fun of him in front of everyone. And what was worse, Brian obviously didn't believe a word Fitz had said.

"Look, Traflon," Brian said angrily, turning back to Fitz. "Nobody bad-mouths Miss Larva and gets away with it. Not even you. Now knock it off."

"But . . . but, Brian . . ." sputtered Fitz.

Brian grabbed Fitz by the front of his shirt. "You

heard me," he said between clenched teeth. "Now *bug off!*"

Fitz's heart was in his throat as he turned and scuffed away. He couldn't believe the way Brian was acting. If his best friend didn't even believe him, who would?

"Hi, Fitz," said a voice behind him. It was Lexi.

"Hi," said Fitz dejectedly.

"What's wrong?" asked Lexi.

Fitz stared at her for a moment. Lexi had seen Miss Larva's eyes. Maybe she'd believe him. "Miss Buggy is making lasagna for lunch, except it isn't really lasagna," he told her.

"What do you mean?" asked Lexi. "How can it be lasagna if it isn't lasagna?"

"It's got caterpillars in it," said Fitz. "They're covered with tomato sauce and mozzarella cheese. I was in the kitchen—I saw her making it."

Lexi gasped. "Gross! But why do you think she would put caterpillars in the lasagna?"

Fitz took a deep breath. Lexi believed him! Just knowing that made him feel a little better. He shrugged. "I don't know. All I know is they were big and fat and green and yellow and black-and-white-striped."

"Yuck!" said Lexi. "I never thought I'd be glad I've got allergies. Are you going to buy your lunch today like you said you would?"

"I don't know," said Fitz. "I didn't bring my lunch, so I guess I don't have much of a choice."

"Well, I don't think you should do it," said Lexi. "We don't know what Miss Buggy is up to."

Fitz smiled in spite of his fear. For once a girl was making sense. "I don't know what I'm going to do," he said. "I think I should try buying lunch to see if it looks suspicious or anything. But I'm not going to eat anything that looks like a caterpillar, that's for sure."

"Fitz," Lexi said softly, "do Miss Buggy's eyes really look like fly's eyes, or did we just imagine it?"

Fitz shook his head. "We didn't imagine it."

Lexi gulped. "I didn't think so. She scares me, Fitz."

"Me, too," he said before he could stop himself. He was afraid Lexi would make fun of him for admitting it, but she didn't.

"Just be careful, okay?" was all she said.

Fitz nodded. His shoulders sagged as he trudged away. Finding out that Lexi believed him had made him feel better for a minute—but only for a minute. Just because she believed him didn't mean anybody else would. And it didn't mean they'd be able to stop Miss Larva from—well, from whatever strange plan she was hatching.

Fitz didn't hear anything his teachers said for the rest of the morning. All he could think about was that pan of lasagna he'd seen bubbling and writhing as Miss Larva put it into the oven. He kept reaching into his jeans pocket to jingle his lunch money in his hand. What was he going to do?

I'll skip lunch, he thought, remembering those wiggling larvae.

He was trudging down the hall after the lunch bell rang when Brian grabbed him from behind.

"Come on, Fitz. You're buying your lunch today, remember?"

Fitz scowled at him. "I'm not hungry, okay?"

"That'll be the day," Brian scoffed. "You're always hungry. Now let's go eat some caterpillars!" He threw back his head and laughed as if that were the funniest thing anybody had ever said.

Then he grabbed Fitz's arm and dragged him through the lunchroom doors. Fitz started to protest, but then he decided to relax and go along with Brian, at least for the moment. He figured he should at least see what Miss Larva was serving that day. If it was meat loaf or pizza or something, that would prove that Fitz had imagined the whole thing, or that the cook had been teasing him. But if it was lasagna . . .

He gritted his teeth and stood on his toes as he tried to see the steam table around the long line of kids. His stomach was churning.

Let it be hamburgers today, he prayed silently,

55

*or tacos, or meatball sandwiches—anything but
lasagna.*

Just then the line shifted and he could see the
steam table clearly. And he could see what was on it.

It was a big pan filled with steaming, bubbling lasagna.

Chapter

Miss Larva was cutting the gigantic pan of lasagna into squares and dishing it up onto plates. Kids pushed and shoved in the line, trying to make it move faster.

All except Fitz. More than anything, he wanted to break out of the line and run away. But for some reason he suddenly found himself unable to move. He was almost paralyzed by the delicious aroma drifting toward him from the steam table, and it kept drawing him closer and closer. The lasagna smelled better to him than anything he had ever smelled in his life. He didn't want to eat it, but he wasn't sure he'd be able to resist that incredible smell. His only hope was that Miss Larva would run out before he got there.

She didn't.

"Here you are, Fitzgerald," she said when Fitz got to the steam table. She gave him a big smile. "Enjoy!"

He looked down at the plate of food on his tray. The piece of lasagna was at least six inches high, and so big that it covered the entire plate and dripped off the edges onto the tray. Holding the tray away from him as far as his arms would reach, Fitz headed for the table. Brian was already there. He was gobbling down his lasagna and grinning at Fitz.

"Hey, I thought we were having bugs for lunch," Brian said.

Fitz didn't answer. He was studying his piece of lasagna carefully. He picked up his fork and poked at it. He could see that it had noodles and meat in it. And tomato sauce and cheese. Just like regular lasagna. He couldn't see any signs of larvae. Nothing green, or purple, or yellow, or black-and-white-striped. Nothing slimy. Nothing pulsating or wiggling. Nothing alive.

He frowned. *How could I have imagined what happened in the kitchen?* he wondered. *She put caterpillars in this! I saw it!*

Fitz looked around the crowded cafeteria. Everyone was gulping down the lasagna as fast as they could, hardly bothering to chew. A few kids were already going back for a second helping.

"What are you waiting for?" asked Brian. "Go

ahead. Take a bite. It's fantastic!"

Fitz looked around again. He was the only person in the whole room who wasn't eating lasagna, except for Lexi, who was nibbling salad out of a plastic container.

The lasagna smelled so good that he was having trouble thinking straight. He poked at it with the end of his fork, then scooped up a tiny piece. He touched it with the tip of his tongue. It was unlike anything he'd ever tasted—he couldn't have even imagined food that good. He closed his eyes and savored it.

Then, taking a deep breath, he put a forkful into his mouth. He started chewing furiously. He could feel his face glowing with pleasure.

He took another bite. And another. He shoveled heaps of lasagna into his mouth.

Just then, out of the corner of his eye, he noticed Miss Larva. She was still behind the steam table dishing up lasagna. But she was staring straight at him. He stared back, still chewing.

Her lips slowly curled into a sneer.

Chapter

A t first Fitz was sure the lasagna was going to make him sick. All afternoon he was on alert for any strange noises coming from his stomach. Or the slightest sign of nausea. Or even the tiniest bit of queasiness.

But nothing happened. He felt perfectly fine. In fact, by the time school let out for the day, he was hungry again. All he could think about was how great it would be to eat some more of Miss Larva's delicious lasagna.

He was positive he had seen caterpillars in the lasagna. Had she thrown away the pan full of caterpillars and substituted regular lasagna after he'd left the kitchen? She must have. But why?

"So what's it going to be tomorrow? Cafeteria food or a soggy sandwich from home?" asked Brian with a grin as they walked home after school.

"I guess I'll give the cafeteria a second try," Fitz mumbled, still thinking about how good that lasagna had tasted.

"I told you so!" Brian said triumphantly. "Miss Larva has to be the best cook in the world. Doesn't she? Come on, say it."

"She's pretty good," said Fitz, frowning.

But Brian wouldn't let it go. "Come on, Traflon. Say it! Miss Larva's the best cook in the world."

"I *said* she's pretty good," Fitz grumbled. "That's as much as I'm going to say right now."

When he went to bed that night, Fitz dreamed about Miss Larva's lasagna. He saw everything just the way it had been that morning in the cafeteria. He saw the larvae squirming and crawling in the red sauce. He saw the cook's round, pudgy face grinning at him as she held up a fat, wiggling larva dripping with sauce and melted cheese—and shoved it into his mouth.

He awoke in a sweat. *It was just a dream,* he told himself. But he had a hard time falling back to sleep.

By the time he was dressed for school, the memory of the dream had faded. All Fitz could think about was how good that lasagna had tasted the day before. The cornflakes he choked down for breakfast tasted like sawdust—all he wanted was some more of Miss Larva's wonderful cooking. He decided to buy his lunch again that day. After all, he'd eaten the lasagna yesterday and nothing bad had happened.

When lunchtime came, Fitz raced Brian to the lunch line, beating him by a fraction of an inch.

"Can you see what we're having?" Brian asked from behind him. "It smells like garlic."

Fitz craned his neck to see the steam tables. His mouth was watering like crazy. "Spaghetti and meatballs! My absolute favorite!" he exclaimed with a grin.

"Awesome," Brian cried. The boys exchanged high fives.

Fitz licked his lips as he watched Miss Larva load his plate with spaghetti. She plopped two gigantic meatballs on top and drowned the whole thing with extra sauce. Then she gave him a massive hunk of garlic bread.

"Could I have another meatball?" Fitz asked.

Miss Larva smiled and put another meatball on his plate. "Of course," she said. "I like to see a boy with a healthy appetite."

Fitz's appetite was humongous. As soon as he sat down he started shoveling the food into his mouth. He hardly noticed the sauce slopping onto his shirt or the long strands of spaghetti dangling down his chin.

"That was even better than the lasagna," he said

to Brian as he picked up the plate and licked off the last speck of sauce. "Come on, let's get some more."

This time Fitz started gorging himself before he even got back to the table. He shoved a meatball into his mouth with his fingers and raced across the lunchroom.

Five minutes later he was back for a third helping. By this time he had decided that eating with a fork was just slowing him down. Grabbing a handful of spaghetti, he stuffed it into his mouth and then licked the sauce off his fingers.

Across the table Brian was eating with his hands, too. He looked up at Fitz and grinned. "Hey, man," Brian said, "you've got so much red stuff around your mouth that you look like a girl." Then in a loud voice he sang, "Fitz is wearing lipstick! Fitz is wearing lipstick!"

Just as Fitz swallowed the food in his mouth and opened it to respond, Brian reached across the table and grabbed a handful of spaghetti off Fitz's plate and stuffed it into his own mouth.

"Hey, what do you think you're doing?" demanded Fitz. Then he grabbed a handful of spaghetti off Brian's plate and ate it.

"Food fight! Food fight!" someone yelled. Suddenly kids all over the lunchroom were jumping up from their tables and racing around grabbing other kids' food. Some of them ate it. Some threw it in other kids' hair or smeared it onto other kids' faces and shirts.

Someone threw a meatball that hit Fitz in the side of the head. He picked it up off the floor and shoved it into his mouth.

The cafeteria was in chaos. Spaghetti and garlic bread were flying everywhere. Meatballs were whizzing in every direction.

Suddenly Fitz froze in the act of flinging a handful of spaghetti at Margie Maxwell. "Look, Brian!" he gasped. "Look at the teachers!" He watched in shock as Mrs. Dewberry drew back her arm and fired a meatball right at the principal's forehead.

Suddenly Fitz noticed Miss Larva and a chill ran down his spine.

She was standing behind the steam table again, watching it all with a huge smile on her face.

Chapter

The next morning Fitz was walking along a block from school, wondering what Miss Larva would fix for lunch that day.

"Wait up, Fitz," he heard Brian call. "I've gotta show you something. Something important." He looked scared.

"What's the matter?" asked Fitz.

Brian didn't answer. Instead he ducked behind a tree and unbuttoned his shirt. He glanced around to make sure no one was watching, then pointed to a lump the size of an egg sticking out from his chest. His finger was trembling.

Fitz stared at the lump. "Whoa! Where did that thing come from?"

Brian shrugged. "I don't know. It was there when I woke up this morning."

"Does it hurt?" Fitz asked, leaning a little closer and squinting at the lump. It was pink and its surface was bumpy.

"No, it just feels funny," Brian said nervously. "I wish I knew what it was."

"Did something hit you?" asked Fitz, remembering when he'd gotten hit in the head with a baseball the summer before. He'd had a lump on his head at least as big as Brian's.

"No," said Brian. "Besides, it isn't black-and-blue or anything."

"What did your parents say when you showed it to them?" asked Fitz.

"Get real. I didn't show it to my parents," said Brian, looking even more worried. "I don't want them to know about it until I know how I got it."

"Maybe it's something you ate," said Fitz. He laughed. Then the memory of the writhing, pulsating larvae in the lasagna pan flashed into his mind and choked off the laugh.

"Feel it," ordered Brian. "It feels weird."

Fitz hesitated and then reached out a finger. The skin was stretched tightly over the lump and it was warm. That was all. He didn't notice anything strange about it. It felt like a plain old ordinary lump. He started to pull his hand away and stopped. Had it moved?

Fitz put his whole hand over the lump. It moved

again! It slowly pulsated and pushed the skin out in first one place and then another.

Fitz gasped and jumped back.

Looking at Brian in horror, he whispered, "It's *alive!*"

Chapter

Neither boy spoke the rest of the way to school. As soon as they got into the building, Fitz motioned for Brian to follow him into the boys' bathroom. There was no one else in there, so Fitz slipped off his shirt.

"Do I have any lumps?" he asked fearfully.

"I don't see any," Brian said with a shrug. "But why would you have one?"

"I don't know. But I don't know why you do, either," said Fitz. "You'll have to admit that things have been pretty weird around school ever since Miss Buggy got here. Maybe it has something to do with her."

"Aw, come on," said Brian. "Don't start that stuff again. I've got enough real problems without worrying about your imaginary bug-monsters."

Fitz stepped in front of the mirror and examined himself closely. There were no signs of any lumps on his chest. He turned, checking his side and back. Then he turned the other side toward the mirror.

"So far, so good," he whispered. He wasn't sure why he felt so sure that Brian's lump had something to do with Miss Larva—but he did.

He was still thinking about Brian's mysterious lump in class a little while later when he glanced at Sarah in the seat in front of his. He blinked and looked again, then caught his breath in terror. There was a lump sticking out on the back of her neck!

Fitz squinted and looked closer. The lump was just below Sarah's short, curly blond hair. He stared at it. If it was the same as Brian's, it would move. He stared at it through narrowed eyes, concentrating so hard that everything else in the room was blurred out of his vision. The lump was the only thing he could see.

"Fitzgerald Traflon, what is the capital of Idaho?"

Mrs. Dewberry's words startled him so much that he almost jumped out of his seat. But he still couldn't take his eyes off the lump on Sarah's neck.

"The capital of . . . I think the capital, uh . . ." he stammered. His mind refused to think about Idaho—or any other state, for that matter. All he could think about was that lump.

Suddenly Sarah's lump shivered ever so slightly. Then it gave a definite wiggle.

Fitz's mouth dropped open and his eyes went wide with fright.

"Fitzgerald, are you daydreaming instead of paying attention to the lesson?" Mrs. Dewberry demanded.

"Yes, ma'am . . . I mean, no, ma'am," said Fitz. He finally managed to pull his eyes away from the pulsating lump to look at the teacher. "I'm sorry, Mrs. Dewberry."

She shook her head, then turned away and called on someone else. She didn't even yell at him. That was strange. But then again, Fitz had grown accustomed to strange behavior from his teachers over the past couple of weeks.

When he was sure Mrs. Dewberry wasn't looking at him anymore, Fitz leaned forward and tapped Sarah on the shoulder.

"Did you know you have a lump on your neck?" he whispered.

Sarah whirled around and gave him an angry look. "So what?" she hissed. "Shut up and mind your own beeswax if you know what's good for you!"

Chapter

15

Lunch that day turned out to be liver and onions. Normally Fitz refused to be in the same room with liver and onions. Even the smell made him gag.

But today the smell made his mouth water. When he stepped up to the steam table to be served, he couldn't help thinking how delicious the dark, slimy slabs of meat looked. And he noticed with delight how the rings of onion sitting on top of the meat looked appetizingly like pale, limp worms. He licked his lips in anticipation.

"Yum!" he whispered to himself. He grabbed a tray and tapped his foot impatiently, wishing that the line would move faster.

When he had finally been served, he gobbled down the liver and onions eagerly, loving every bite.

The meat was as tough as the soles of his shoes. Cutting it with his knife and fork only slowed him down. He scooped up the onions and ate them with his fingers. Then he picked up the whole piece of meat and crammed it into his mouth.

He had hardly finished chewing the first helping before he went back for seconds. And thirds.

On his fourth trip to the steam table he grinned at Miss Larva. "This is great. What'd you put in it? Road kill?"

The cook looked up. She peered at him through her dark sunglasses. He imagined he could make out all the tiny irises in her eyes behind the glasses. They all seemed to be focusing on him.

"Were you spying on me again?" she demanded angrily.

"No way!" Fitz protested. "I was just making a joke. Honest."

Suddenly someone jerked him roughly from behind. Fitz spun around and came face-to-face with his best friend. Brian's face was blazing with anger.

"What's the big idea?" he screamed. "You're making Miss Larva mad! I don't like that! Got it?"

Fitz's mouth dropped open in amazement. He couldn't believe what was coming out of his best friend's mouth. Brian had never yelled at him that way before.

"Brian, no kidding. I was just making a joke," Fitz insisted.

Brian shoved him against the wall. Putting his face close to Fitz's, he growled, "You dirtbag. Make a joke like that about Miss Larva again, and I'll beat you to a pulp."

Suddenly other angry kids were swarming around Fitz and Brian.

"Leave Miss Larva alone, you big creep," shouted Sarah.

"Yeah, you better watch what you say, you loser," added Jeff McCormick.

He and Brian were advancing toward Fitz from one side. Jimmy Forsyth was leading an angry group from the other direction.

Fitz gulped and took a step backward. He could see the lump on Brian's chest sticking out from beneath the collar of his shirt.

It had grown! It was at least double the size it had been that morning.

And what was that bulge under Jeff's shirt? Fitz could hardly believe his eyes. It was a lump—just like the ones Brian and Sarah had.

Then Fitz noticed something else. As his angry classmates advanced on him, threatening looks on their faces, all three of the lumps were pulsating faster and faster. *As if they were excited!*

Chapter

itz raced down the hall. His heart was pounding even faster than his feet. Ducking into an empty classroom, he could hear the mob of kids coming after him. He crouched down in a corner and held his breath as the angry shouts came closer and closer.

Suddenly the door opened and Brian's head popped into the room.

Fitz froze, afraid to move, as Brian made a quick survey of the room. Luckily he didn't notice Fitz huddled in the dark corner.

"He's not in here," Brian called out. His head disappeared again.

Fitz breathed a sigh of relief as he heard the crowd moving on down the hall.

"What's the matter with everybody?" he whispered to himself. "They've all gone berserk!"

Fitz hid out in the empty classroom until the bell rang ending lunch period. He knew he had to go back to his own classroom and face Brian, Sarah, and the others who had turned on him. He was terrified. What if they jumped him again?

Mrs. Dewberry will be there. She won't let them try anything, he thought.

Cautiously he stepped out into the hall. He looked first one way and then the other. Two kids hurried by on their way to their classes. They didn't pay any attention to him.

Tiptoeing along, Fitz suddenly stopped short when he turned the corner and saw Brian leaning against the wall outside their room.

Fitz's heart thumped against his chest. His palms were sweaty. He looked around for a place to hide. But before he could move, Brian spotted him.

A smile spread over Brian's face. "Hey, Fitz. Where have you been? I've been looking all over for you," he called out cheerfully.

Fitz swallowed hard. What was going on now? "Just around," he mumbled uncertainly.

"Man, I don't know what happened to me in the cafeteria," said Brian. He shook his head and frowned as if he were still trying to figure it out. "I didn't want to say those things, but I couldn't help it," he went on. "It was like somebody else was inside my head, talking and acting—and *thinking* for

80

me. Anyway, I just want you to know I'm sorry."

Fitz stared at Brian in horror. The things Brian was saying were supposed to make him feel better.

Instead, they were making him feel worse—a *lot* worse!

Chapter

17

Fitz couldn't understand it. How could some-body—or some*thing*—make Brian say things and do things he didn't want to say or do?

"Hi, Fitz," Sarah said in her usual flirtatious voice as he slid into his seat. She turned around, grinning and batting her eyelashes at him.

Fitz looked at her in surprise. Then he looked around the classroom. All the kids who had made up the angry mob a few minutes ago were now sitting quietly in their seats. No one seemed the least bit angry anymore. The situation was getting crazier by the moment.

"Okay, people. Everybody get into your seat! And *shut up!*" screamed Mrs. Dewberry.

Fitz glanced up in amazement. Even before all the teachers had started acting so nice, Mrs. Dewberry had always been mild-mannered and cheerful. But now there was a wild look in her eyes. Her face was bright red, and her straight brown hair was sticking out every which way, making her look as though she had stuck her finger into a light socket. She was pacing back and forth in front of the class with a nasty look on her face.

"Put away your books," she ordered. "We're going to have a test. *Right now!*"

Meekly Fitz obeyed. So did everybody else. The room was so quiet you could practically hear the dust settle.

Fitz kept his head down and peeked up at Mrs. Dewberry out of the corner of his eye. She was stomping up and down the rows, slapping papers down on the desks.

He jumped when he got his, afraid even to look up at his teacher.

The test was horrible. Fitz read over the first question: *If you have seven bananas and you take away nine eggs, how many frogs do you have left?*

He read it again, then shook his head in frustration. It didn't even make sense!

Across the room Brian raised his hand. "Excuse me, Mrs. Dewberry, but I don't understand the first problem," he said.

The teacher whirled away from the blackboard and glared at Brian. "How dare you open your mouth during a test!" she cried.

"But . . . but . . . I was just asking a question," he protested.

"That's enough smart mouth out of you, young man," the teacher said angrily. "No one talks during a test in *my* class and gets away with it. Go to the principal's office this instant!"

Fitz watched his best friend get slowly to his feet and scuff out the door, a look of disbelief on his face.

Fitz struggled over the problems, doing the best he could. None of them made any more sense than the first one. But he didn't dare raise his hand after what had happened to Brian. Instead, he just guessed at the answers.

The second part of the test looked like algebra. He frowned and scratched his head in confusion. They hadn't even studied that stuff yet. How could Mrs. Dewberry put something on the test that they hadn't studied? But he kept his mouth shut.

Mrs. Dewberry gave them only ten minutes to finish the test. When she collected the tests, she announced, "Your homework for tonight is to read pages nineteen through eighty-five in your textbook and do all the problems."

Fitz cringed. *Pages nineteen through eighty-five! That's almost half the book!*

He ducked down behind Sarah and studied his

teacher closely. Mrs. Dewberry was sitting at her desk, grading the test papers. What was happening to her?

"Oh, no," he whispered to himself.

He had just spotted the thing he had dreaded finding.

A lump on the teacher's shoulder was pushing out the fabric of her dress. A big lump that moved, even when she didn't.

Chapter

Lexi caught up with Fitz as he was leaving the building after school.

"I couldn't believe what happened in the cafeteria today," she said. "It was freaky, all those kids picking on you like that."

"Tell me about it," grumbled Fitz.

Lexi was silent for a moment as they walked. Then she said, "Fitz, can I ask you something kind of personal?"

He looked at her. "Yeah, I guess."

"Do you have any . . ." She paused and gulped, looking a little embarrassed, but scared at the same time. "Um, do you have any funny bumps on your body?"

Startled, he looked at her closely. "No," he answered slowly. "Why?"

"Sarah does," Lexi said quietly. "And . . . and I was just wondering if anyone else did. Because I was also wondering if Sarah's lump had anything to do with her eating Miss Buggy's cooking. But if you don't have any, then that must not be the reason."

"Why don't you tell her to show it to her parents?" said Fitz.

"I did," said Lexi. "But she went ballistic on me." She shook her head. "She's never yelled at me like that before. It was like she was—I don't know—*possessed* or something. It was weird. But anyway, I guess I don't have to worry. You've been buying your lunch, so if you don't have any lumps, I guess there must be some other explanation."

"I guess so," said Fitz. He watched as Lexi turned the corner toward her house and waved cheerfully. He wasn't sure why he hadn't told her about Brian's lump. Maybe he should have, he thought. Maybe she could have helped him figure the whole thing out. It just felt strange to confide in a girl that way. He shook his head, feeling almost as confused about Lexi as about Miss Larva.

When Fitz reached home, he went straight to his room. He undressed quickly and examined himself all over for lumps. He stood in front of the mirror, inspecting every inch of his body. Then he poked and prodded himself from head to toe, searching for any mysterious growths under his skin.

He breathed a deep sigh of relief. Nothing.

"Wow. Am I ever lucky," he mumbled to himself. He paused and thought for a moment. "So far, at least."

As he was getting dressed again, Fitz heard the phone ringing out in the hall. A moment later his mother called him. "Fitz, it's for you. It's Brian."

Fitz raced to the phone. "Hi, Brian, what's up?"

"Can you come over?" asked Brian. "Right now? I need to talk to you." His voice was low and shaky.

"What's the matter?" Fitz was almost afraid to ask.

"I can't talk about it over the phone," Brian said. "Just get over here *fast*. Okay?"

"Sure," said Fitz. "I'll be there in a minute."

He grabbed his jacket and ran the three blocks to Brian's house. The front door flew open as soon as Fitz turned up the sidewalk, and Brian motioned for him to come in.

"What's the big emergency?" Fitz asked as Brian closed his bedroom door behind them.

Brian's hands were shaking as he peeled off his shirt. "Look," he said, turning his back to Fitz.

Fitz's eyes opened wide with alarm. "Oh, no. Another lump!" he cried. "When did you find it?"

"Right before I called you. My back felt funny, so I

took off my shirt to look. What am I going to do, Fitz?"

"I dunno," said Fitz. He reached out and poked the second lump. It was a lot smaller than the one on Brian's chest. But it was warm. And it was moving slightly under his skin.

"It's awful," said Brian. "And the lumps aren't the only weird thing that's happening to me these days. Sometimes things come over me that I can't fight off. Like today in the cafeteria—I knew you were making a joke. But it was as if there was another person inside me. Controlling me. Making me say things I didn't want to say. And do things I didn't want to do."

"What do you mean?" asked Fitz.

"It's really bizarre. Sometimes I think I can hear voices," said Brian. He paused and shook his head. "No . . . not voices exactly. It's more like someone else's *thoughts* are in my *head*. Fitz, you've got to help me!" There was fear in his eyes. "I don't know what to do."

Fitz swallowed hard. "I think you'd better tell your parents," he said.

"No," Brian insisted. "I can't. What if they take me to the doctor and he finds out I've got something awful? Something—terminal?"

"Brian, listen to me," said Fitz, grabbing Brian by the shoulders. "I saw a lump on the back of Sarah's neck this morning."

90

Brian eyed him nervously. "So? What's that supposed to mean?"

"It means you're not the only one. I also saw a lump on Mrs. Dewberry's shoulder when she was giving us that awful test," said Fitz. "Don't you get it? I think it may all be connected to Miss Buggy in some way. You've got to go to the doctor. We can't figure out what to do about it until we know what it is!"

Suddenly Brian's face changed. He looked furious. "*Didn't you hear me?* I said forget it! And for the last time, it's Miss *Larva*. Now get off my back, Traflon."

Fitz held up his hands in surrender as he backed away from his angry friend. He realized that whatever strange mood had come over his friend earlier had returned. "Okay, okay. I was only trying to help."

Brian glared at him and balled his hands into fists. Fitz left without another word.

When Fitz got home a little while later, he was more scared than ever. Something terrible was going on. And it was getting worse all the time.

He went to his room and closed the door. Standing in front of the mirror, he took off his shirt. He had to check again, even though it had been less than an hour since he had last looked for lumps. He had to know if his luck was still holding out.

Fitz squinted first at his chest and stomach, running his fingers over them carefully. Then his arms, turning them so that he could see all the way around each one.

And then his eyes bugged out in horror.

He saw it.

A tiny lump, growing on his left side.

Chapter

Fitz couldn't sleep at all that night. All he could do was stare at the ceiling and worry about the horrible thing growing on his body. Each time he turned onto his left side, he could feel the lump throb. It felt as if the lump were demanding more space.

By morning the lump had grown to the size of a Ping-Pong ball and felt warm. For the millionth time since he'd found it, Fitz cupped his hand over it and felt it moving.

Fitz threw on his clothes and left for school without eating breakfast or saying good morning to his parents. There was something he had to know—and only one person could give him the information he needed.

He ran all the way to school. He barely slowed

down as he burst through the wide front doors and sprinted down the hall to the cafeteria. This time he didn't sneak in on tiptoe. He pushed open the door to the kitchen and boldly strode inside.

"Miss Larva, I have a question about insects," he said loudly.

The cook was mixing something in a large bowl. At the sound of his voice she turned around and smiled. "Certainly, Fitzgerald," she said in a lilting voice. "I'm always glad to help a child who's *hungry* for knowledge. Hee hee. What is your question?"

Fitz hesitated an instant. Now that the moment had come, he was almost afraid to ask. But at the same time, he had to know the answer.

"When I came in here before, you said that all insects go through four stages to become an adult, and that being a larva was stage two. My question is—what is stage three?"

Miss Larva put down her spoon and looked at him thoughtfully. "Stage three is when the larva makes a pupa or a cocoon. A cocoon is a sort of nest where the insect can burrow in and be warm and well fed and where it can grow. Then, when it's finished growing to its adult size, it will go into stage four."

"What's stage four?" asked Fitz.

"That's the best stage of all," said Miss Larva. "That's when it bursts out of its cocoon and becomes the beautiful creature it was meant to be."

She let out a sigh of ecstasy and rolled her eyes toward the ceiling. "The whole process is known as metamorphosis! Isn't it wonderful?"

"But what happens to the cocoon?" Fitz asked, his voice barely louder than a whisper.

"The cocoon?" asked Miss Larva in surprise. Then a nasty smile spread across her face. "When the insect hatches, it no longer has any use for it. So the cocoon withers up and dies."

Fitz stared at her in terror.

Now he knew the awful truth.

He finally understood what was happening to him and his friends.

Chapter

Fitz ran out of the building like a bullet shot from a gun. He had to find Brian and tell him what he'd learned.

Kids were just starting to arrive at school. Some were walking. Others were pouring off the buses parked at the curb. Sarah waved at him from across the playground. He ignored her and kept looking for Brian. It took him another minute or two to locate his best friend by the bike rack.

"Brian! I've got to talk to you!" Fitz yelled, racing toward him. Pulling Brian over to a deserted corner of the playground, he whispered hoarsely, "I just talked to Miss Buggy, and I've got it all figured out. Oh, man, you're not going to believe this!"

"What are you talking about?" asked Brian.

"She put larvae into our food and turned all of

us into living, breathing, walking-around *cocoons*!" Fitz cried.

"What are you talking about, dude?" Brian said, looking confused. "You talked to Miss Larva? And what do you mean by cocoons?"

Fitz took a deep breath. He had to convince Brian that what he was saying was true. "You know those lumps of yours? You know how Sarah and Jeff and Mrs. Dewberry have them, too? Well, now I've got one."

Brian's eyes widened. "No kidding?"

"No kidding," Fitz said solemnly.

"But what does that have to do with Miss Larva?"

"Well, you know how the lumps are kind of warm?" Fitz said. "And you know how they move around—like there's something *alive* inside of them?"

Brian nodded.

"Think about it," Fitz said urgently. "Miss Buggy is always talking about bugs, right? Well, she told me that one of the stages in a bug's life is burrowing into a cocoon—you know, a warm, cozy place where it can grow. And the next stage is *bursting out* of it."

Brian's mouth dropped open. "You mean, we've got bugs growing inside our bodies? That's what those lumps are? *We're* cocoons?"

Fitz nodded. "I wasn't imagining things the

day I saw caterpillars in the lasagna."

"I should have believed you," said Brian, shaking his head. "You're my best friend. I really should have believed you. But do you know how bizarre that story sounded?"

"Yeah, I know. It seemed pretty bizarre to me, too, and I was there," said Fitz. "But anyway, we've got bigger problems now. Miss Buggy also told me that after the bugs burst out of the cocoon, the cocoon withers up and dies."

"You mean—you mean that's what's going to happen to us?" Brian asked, his face paling. "All of us?"

Fitz just nodded. Neither of them said anything for a moment.

Then Brian shook his head. "Hey, man, I'm sorry about jumping on you last night. If only I'd known . . ."

"Forget it," said Fitz. "Just try to hold off whatever's making you act that way until we can figure out what to do."

"I'll try," said Brian. "You know, this must have been what Miss Larva meant that day she showed us her experiments and told us we were going to be part of her biggest one."

"Yeah," said Fitz. "Who knew we'd be the ones she was experimenting on? Anyway, I don't think we have much time. The lumps are growing fast. It's up to you and me to figure out a way to destroy whatever's in them before it destroys us."

Brian's eyes narrowed menacingly. Then his face twisted, as if he were fighting something. "No, I . . . I . . . leave me out of this, you stupid creep," he suddenly spat out. "You make me want to puke!"

He whirled around and stomped away.

Fitz watched him go. Fear clogged his throat and choked off his breath. It had happened again. Whatever the terrible things were that were growing inside them, they were in control of Brian again.

Slowly, Fitz realized that it was all going to be up to him. He had been the last one to eat the cafeteria food, so the things hadn't had as much time to grow inside him—they weren't powerful enough to take him over yet. But they would be soon. And then Fitz wouldn't be able to help Brian or himself or anybody. He didn't know how much time he had.

He had to do something fast. But what?

Chapter

F itz vowed that he wasn't going to eat Miss Larva's cooking anymore. Before leaving for school on Monday, he made himself a triple-decker ham-and-cheese sandwich with mustard and onions—one of his favorites. But when lunchtime came, the aroma that filled the cafeteria was so appetizing that he tossed the sandwich into the trash can and borrowed money from Brian to pay for lunch.

He gobbled up everything Miss Larva served as if it were going out of style. He loved the cooked carrots and broccoli and the boiled cabbage. He devoured the bird's-nest soup, goat cheese, and pickled pig's feet.

"Save room for dessert," she said sweetly as he came back for a sixth serving. "I fixed fried-brains pudding. It's my specialty. It will be out of the oven shortly."

Yum! thought Fitz, licking his lips hungrily. *Fried-brains pudding!* He had never tried it, but it sounded delicious.

He waited impatiently for Miss Larva to bring the pudding out of the kitchen. He drummed his fingertips on the table. He was so ravenously hungry that he was tempted to go back for another helping of pickled pig's feet just to tide him over.

"What are you doing in there?" he shouted impatiently. "Bring on the fried-brains pudding! Bring on the fried-brains pudding!"

Brian joined the chant. "Bring on the fried-brains pudding! Bring on the fried-brains pudding!"

Pretty soon the entire cafeteria was chanting and banging their spoons on the tables.

Finally the kitchen door swung open and Miss Larva marched out, carrying an enormous pan filled with what looked like pale-gray scrambled eggs. A strange but fascinating smell filled the air.

"Here it is, everyone," sang Miss Larva. "What you've all been waiting for. My fried-brains pudding."

Fitz pushed and shoved his way to the front of the line. His mouth watered as he carried the bowl of slimy, runny pudding back to his table.

When he finally tasted it, he almost couldn't believe how good it was. He held the first bite in his mouth for a long time, savoring the sickly sweet taste.

Miss Buggy's cooking is terrific! She's the best

102

cook in the world! More! More! he thought.

Then suddenly he realized those weren't his thoughts at all.

They were the thoughts of something inside him!

Chapter

Voices woke Fitz in the middle of the night.

He couldn't make out what they were saying. But they were voices all right, and they were right there in his room. Little prickles of fear ran across his scalp and down his spine.

He peered into the darkness. Nothing moved.

I can't be hearing voices, he told himself.

Then he heard them again. Soft, whispery voices.

He strained, listening as hard as he could. Suddenly he realized that the voices weren't in his room at all.

They were in his head.

"Fitzgerald Traflon the Third," came a dry, rustling whisper. It was like the sound of leaves scuttling across a sidewalk. "We can make you do anything we want you to do. *You are ours.*"

105

Fitz put his hands over his ears, trying to stop the voices.

"You are ours! You are ours!" The voices swirled in his mind, over and over again, until he thought he was going crazy.

Fitz shook his head violently from side to side. "Who are you? What do you want?" he shrieked into the darkness.

The next thing he knew, his bedroom door flew open and light spilled in from the hallway.

"Fitz, are you okay?" his father shouted as he burst into the room.

His mother ran to his bed and put her arms around him. "What's wrong, sweetheart?"

Fitz snuggled into his mother's arms. The rustling whispers were gone—for now. "I—I thought I heard something. Voices," he said.

"Voices, sweetheart?" asked his mother as she stroked his hair. "You must have been dreaming."

"That's right, son," said his father, pulling the door open even farther so that the room was light. "There's no one in here but you. See? No ghosts. No goblins." He pulled back the curtains and opened the closet door, showing Fitz that nothing was there.

Fitz wanted desperately to tell his parents the truth. He wanted to show them the lump growing on his side. He longed to explain to them about the voices in his head that could control him and make him do things he didn't want to do.

He tried to force the words out, but he couldn't.

"Now you forget all about your nightmare and go back to sleep," said his father. "Your mother and I are right across the hall if you need us."

"That's right, sweetie," said his mother, standing up to leave.

Fitz didn't want them to leave. He didn't want to be alone again—with the voices. He tried to call out as his parents headed for the door. His lips moved, but no sound came out.

He watched the door close behind them, feeling lonelier than he had ever felt in his life.

Chapter

By morning the voices had stopped, but a second lump had appeared on Fitz's leg. And the lump on his side had grown even larger.

Fitz knew that time was running out.

I have to find a way to destroy the larvae, he thought as he rubbed the new lump on his leg. *Before they destroy us.*

He kept an eye out for Brian all the way to school. Maybe the two of them could put their brains together and come up with a plan. It was definitely worth a try. He had to do something—and do it fast.

But even after he got to school, he couldn't find Brian anywhere. Fitz had almost given up when he spotted Brian walking toward him across the baseball diamond.

"Hey, Brian! Over here! I've got to talk to you," Fitz shouted.

Brian waved and trotted toward him.

But as Brian got closer, a strange sensation came over Fitz. He suddenly felt boiling mad. His breath was coming out in snorts. His fists were doubling up into hard, round balls.

He was nose-busting mad! By the time Brian reached him, he was ready to explode.

Fitz watched as his own fist shot out and smashed Brian in the face.

Brian reeled back, a look of total surprise on his face. "What the—"

Before he could say another word, Fitz punched him again. He tried not to, but he couldn't seem to stop himself. His arms were flailing like a windmill in a hurricane, and there wasn't a thing he could do about it. The more he punched Brian, the more he wanted to punch him again.

Brian's nose was bleeding by this time, and blood dripped from a cut on his lip.

Fitz socked him in the nose once more and watched with satisfaction as Brian went down, sprawling in the dirt. "Serves you right, you jerk," he said with a sneer.

Other kids were rushing over from all directions to watch the fight. Some of them started cheering for Brian. Others yelled for Fitz.

"Hit him, Fitz!" yelled Jimmy Forsyth. "Smash him good!"

"Go get him, Brian!" shouted Eric Plummer. "Beat him up!"

A mean look came into Brian's eyes. He jumped to his feet and started fighting back.

"Hit him, Fitz!" yelled Sarah.

Brian caught Fitz in the mouth with a right. Fitz grabbed Brian around the neck, and the two of them fell to the ground, hitting and kicking and pounding on each other. They rolled over and over in the dirt.

Gradually the blows began to slow down. Fitz was getting tired, and so was Brian.

Finally they stopped.

"Aw, come on, guys, fight some more!" yelled Jeff McCormick eagerly.

Brian got up and wiped a mixture of blood, sweat, and dirt off his face. Then he moved off the dusty baseball field and sat down in the grass behind first base, panting hard. The crowd started to drift away. Fitz, exhausted, dropped down onto the grass next to his friend.

As he sat there, the remnants of his anger faded away. He realized that he wasn't mad at Brian anymore. He never really had been. He had never wanted to fight his best friend.

He glanced over at Brian. "I guess it's my turn to be sorry," he said tentatively.

"Don't be," said Brian. "I understand why you did it."

Fitz looked at his friend sadly. *I'm not the one who picked the fight, he thought. I didn't have any more control over it than Brian did when he got mad at me.*

Then the whispers came again, as dry and crisp as the crackling of a fire.

"Fitzgerald Traflon the Third, we told you that you were in our power. Now you know it's true. *Hee hee hee.*"

Chapter

"You are in our power," the voices whispered again.

Fear prickled Fitz's scalp, like a hundred spiders dancing in his hair.

The voices had to be the larvae, he decided. They were not only in his body, they had to be in his brain, too. They could make him think things he didn't want to think and do things he didn't want to do, like slugging Brian.

And when they decided to come out, they wouldn't just come bursting out of his side and his leg. The thought of what else might happen made him shiver.

Fitz got slowly to his feet. His body ached and his head throbbed. Dark bruises were starting to appear on his arms and knuckles.

Just then Lexi came over. She looked scared. "What happened? Why were you two fighting like that?"

"Do you remember when you asked me if I had any lumps on my body, and I said no?" asked Fitz.

Lexi nodded.

"Well, I do now," said Fitz. "And so does everyone else, including Mrs. Dewberry. I'll bet Mr. Gladstone and the other teachers have them, too. Everybody has them but you. You're the only one who has escaped, and do you know why?"

Lexi looked from Fitz to Brian and then back to Fitz. "Because I haven't eaten any cafeteria food," she whispered, her voice so low that the boys could hardly hear her.

Fitz nodded grimly. "I know it sounds crazy, but Miss Buggy is putting larvae in the food, and the larvae are using us as cocoons so they can grow."

"But that's impossible," Lexi insisted, shaking her head. "I mean, I know she's weird, but . . ." Her voice trailed off and her eyes widened. "The experiment! She told us that day in the cafeteria that we'd all be part of her big experiment."

"You've got it," said Fitz. "That's why Sarah has been acting so mean toward you lately. And that's why Brian and I were fighting. The larvae are taking control of our bodies and making us do all kinds of strange things."

"And it's getting worse," said Brian in a panicky voice. "It's getting worse *fast*. What are we going to do?"

"That's what I wanted to talk to you about when I slugged you," Fitz said. "I think we should come up with as many ideas as we can to fight this thing. You too, Lexi. We need your help. Let's think during school today. Then after school we can get together again to figure out which ideas are the best."

"I can't do it after school today," Lexi said. "I have my weekly appointment with my allergist."

"I can't make it today either," said Brian. "My mom says I have to come straight home and clean out the garage. I've been putting it off all week—if I don't do it today, she'll kill me."

Fitz gritted his teeth. With things getting so bad, even one day's delay seemed too long. But there was nothing he could do about it. "Okay, how about tomorrow morning?" he suggested. "The three of us could meet here on the playground."

"Cool," said Brian. "I'll be here."

"Me, too," Lexi promised.

Fitz had trouble sleeping again that night. He couldn't come up with any ideas for getting rid of the larvae. And every time he snuggled down in his bed and got comfortable, the lumps started throbbing furiously. Then the dry, crackling voices started up again. They were faint and far away.

They seemed to be talking to each other inside his head.

Fitz listened hard over the terrified thumping of his heart. He wanted desperately to know what the voices were saying, but they were speaking too softly for him to hear.

He took a couple of deep breaths. That calmed him a little, and his heart seemed to beat a little more quietly. He strained to listen again.

Finally, coming so faintly that he wasn't sure if he really heard them, were two words.

"... *Fitzgerald* ..."

"... soon ..."

Chapter

"I sure hope you've thought of a good plan, because I haven't," Fitz said when he met Brian and Lexi at the playground.

Brian grinned. "Have I ever," he said. He was carrying a small paper bag. He reached in and drew out a bottle. "It's liquid insect poison. I found it in our garage," he said. "One sip of this, and they're *zapped!*"

Lexi gave him a disgusted look. "Are you crazy? One sip of that stuff and *you'll* be zapped. You can't drink poison."

For a second Brian looked angry. Then his expression changed to embarrassment as he realized Lexi was right. "Oh, yeah. I guess I wasn't thinking," he said quietly. "So do you guys have any ideas?"

Lexi shook her head. "I've been thinking about it nonstop, but I can't think of a thing," she admitted.

Fitz was eyeing the bottle of poison. "What do you think would happen if we rubbed some of that stuff on the lumps? Do you suppose it would soak into the skin and kill them that way?"

Brian gave him a skeptical look. "I don't know." He handed the bottle to Fitz. "But it's your idea. Here, you try it."

"I don't know about this," Lexi said uncertainly. "It seems kind of dangerous. You could end up burning off your skin or something."

Fitz shrugged. "We've got to try something." He took the bottle and set it on the ground beside him. Then he unbuttoned his shirt and picked up the bottle again. The lump on his side was the size of a grapefruit half. It was quiet now, as if the larvae inside were asleep.

He hesitated and looked at Brian. "Maybe Lexi's right. Maybe this isn't such a good idea after all," he said.

"Go ahead," urged Brian. "Who knows? It might work."

Fitz took a deep breath and unscrewed the top of the bottle. He sniffed the poison and wrinkled his nose. It smelled awful.

Suddenly a weird and powerful force seemed to take over his vocal cords. He let out a piercing scream that was so loud that Brian and Lexi jumped in surprise. Fitz looked down at the lump on his side. It was pulsating like crazy. The throbbing was getting stronger by the second, pushing and pulling and pounding his insides. Fitz had to lean against a tree to keep himself from falling down.

"I didn't even touch it with that stuff!" Fitz exclaimed as soon as the lump calmed down enough for him to speak. "All I did was open the bottle. But it knew. It knew exactly what I was going to do!"

"Yeah," said Lexi, her voice shaky. "It's as if it could read your mind."

"I wonder what would happen if we tried to cut the lumps out," Brian said.

Fitz shuddered at the thought. "Ouch," he said. "Hey, I know. Maybe we could make tiny little slits in the tops of the lumps and squeeze them like big pimples."

"Oh, ugh," said Lexi, her face turning a little green.

"Hey, yeah," said Brian. He made a loud popping sound with his mouth. "We could pop them like zits!"

"Gross!" moaned Lexi. "You guys are making me sick. Anyway, don't you think that would hurt pretty bad, too?"

"I guess it would," agreed Fitz. Suddenly he didn't like the idea so well himself. "Maybe we can come up with a better plan if we keep trying."

"All right, but we should hurry," Lexi warned. "We don't know how much time we have before those things explode." She shuddered. "I may not have any myself, but I sure don't want to be around to see everybody else's hatch. That's for sure."

Fitz didn't want to think about that, but he knew Lexi was right. They had to hurry. He glanced toward the school building. "What if we sneak into the school and look around in Miss Buggy's kitchen?" he suggested.

"What good would that do?" asked Lexi. "I don't want to go near that place."

"Why not? Maybe we'll find some kind of clue. Miss Buggy won't be expecting us to go into the cafeteria. Maybe she left some notes on her experiments lying around."

"Great idea, man!" said Brian. "They might even tell how to kill the larvae."

"Yeah," said Fitz. He closed his eyes and imagined his skin tearing open and giant insects bursting out of his side and his leg and crawling out his mouth. He could almost feel the searing pain and smell the awful stench. "Before they kill us," he murmured.

"Well, all right. But how are we going to get in?" asked Lexi. "They keep the school locked up on the weekend."

Fitz scratched his head and thought for a minute. "Let's go around back," he suggested. "There's a door leading straight into the kitchen. It's where delivery trucks bring in the food for the cafeteria. Maybe we can get in there somehow."

The trio hurried around the school. The door at the back was closed. But to their surprise it unlatched with a click when Fitz turned the knob. He pushed the door slightly ajar.

"If my parents could see me now," Lexi commented. "Breaking and entering."

Fitz ignored her. He was nervous enough already without any help from Lexi. "Ready?" he whispered.

Brian looked anxiously at the door for a second and then nodded. "I'm with you, dude."

"I'm not sure I like this," said Lexi. Her voice was trembling again.

"You could stay out here and be our lookout, Lexi," Fitz offered.

"Gladly," she said, looking relieved.

Fitz pushed the door all the way open and the two boys slipped inside. They tiptoed cautiously into the silent kitchen and stood in the middle of the room, looking around. Everything seemed to be in perfect order, scrubbed and shined.

Where would Miss Buggy keep the notes on her experiments? Fitz wondered. He glanced first toward the cabinets and then toward the drawers.

Suddenly Fitz heard a loud click behind him. He exchanged panicky glances with Brian. They whirled around together and gasped.

They were face-to-face with Miss Larva.

She was blocking the door, her hand on the lock. She had taken off her dark glasses, and her sinister insect eyes had grown even larger. They were bulging out hideously, covering more than half her face. Every facet of every eye was staring straight at the boys.

"Brian Collins and Fitzgerald Traflon the Third," she rasped, "my friends told me you might try something like this. I've been waiting for you in the storage room." She threw back her head and cackled wildly. "I have you in my power now. *You'll never escape!*"

Chapter

Suddenly Fitz heard a sound coming from the other side of the door.

"Fitz! Brian! Are you in there?" It was Lexi, and she sounded scared.

"Run, Lexi!" Fitz cried. "Go for help! Miss Buggy's got us trapped!"

Like a flash of lightning, the cook whirled and threw open the door, grabbing the startled girl and dragging her inside.

"Let her go!" screamed Fitz. "She's not a cocoon! She never eats in the cafeteria. She has too many allergies."

"Don't hurt her," Brian added. "It's us you want."

Suddenly Miss Larva's expression changed. The evil look faded away. A smile spread slowly across her face. She loosened her grip on Lexi, who stumbled across the room and collapsed against the counter beside the boys.

"What's she going to do?" Lexi whispered. Tears brimmed in her eyes.

Miss Larva turned and locked the door. Then she held up the keys for the kids to see before she dropped them into her apron pocket.

"Are you children hungry?" she asked sweetly. "I'm famished. Why don't I just whip up a little something for us to eat?"

Food! thought Fitz. *That's the worst thing she could do!*

But he realized it was part of her plan. She knew that neither he nor Brian would be able to resist her cooking. And the more she fed them, the faster the larvae would grow—until they finally grew large enough to burst out of their cocoons. She really did have them in her power.

"Come on, guys," Fitz whispered to his friends. "Let's make a break for it." He was desperate. He was ready to try anything.

He skidded across the kitchen to the swinging double doors leading into the lunchroom. Brian and Lexi were right behind him. All three shoved as hard as they could with their shoulders.

The doors didn't budge. They were locked tight.

Fitz turned around, panting, and leaned against

them. He looked around frantically for another way out.

There wasn't any.

"Ladybug, Ladybug, fly away home," sang Miss Larva as she busily pressed ground meat into hamburger patties and sliced potatoes into french fries. She worked like a whirlwind, and soon the smell of grilling hamburgers filled the room.

Fitz watched in horror as she cooked. His mouth watered from the heavenly smell. He could feel himself weakening. Suddenly, escaping just didn't seem as important anymore. The most important thing he could think of was sinking his teeth into one of those delicious, juicy burgers. He could almost taste it already. The room was starting to spin.

No! I can't eat anything, Fitz told himself. *I can't!*

"But you'll love it," said a voice inside him.

"Just one tiny bite," said another voice.

I'm so hungry. Just one bite, then I'll try to find a way out of here again, he told himself.

NO! That's not me thinking that! Fitz shouted to himself.

Miss Larva glanced at Fitz and smiled. "I've got to feed my little pets, now, don't I?" she asked with a sinister cackle.

Beside him Lexi started to cry.

I have to keep a clear head, Fitz warned himself.

He fought to push away the voices that were rising inside him.

Then he noticed Brian standing beside the stove, gazing down at the french fries bubbling in the grease. He was licking his lips hungrily.

Fitz closed his eyes to shut out the sight of the food. He had to get hold of himself before it was too late.

Maybe the three of us can overpower her and get the key, he thought. *All I have to do is get Brian's attention away from the french fries.*

"Psst. Brian," he called softly.

At the same instant, Miss Larva whipped three plates out of the cupboard. In the blink of an eye she loaded four hamburgers and a gigantic helping of french fries on each one. Then she passed the plates under their noses.

"Lunch is ready, children," she cooed sweetly.

Fitz and Brian followed her like a pair of zombies. It was as if the delicious aroma was pulling them across the floor.

Only Lexi didn't follow Miss Larva. Fitz was vaguely aware that she was still cringing by the counter, but he was powerless to do anything but trail after the cook.

Before the plates could even touch the counter, Fitz had grabbed one of the burgers and stuffed it into his mouth.

"Mmm, delicious. How about some ketchup?" he asked around a gigantic bite.

"Yeah. And some mustard, too," Brian added between bites. French fries stuck out of his mouth every which way.

Miss Larva had been about to open a cupboard. Her hand stopped in midair, and she glared at Brian.

"You *know* I don't allow mustard in my lunchroom!" she bellowed.

"But that's stupid," said Fitz, his mouth full. "Why not?"

Miss Larva glared at Fitz. Each one of the hundreds of tiny eyes within her pupils held a fiery glitter.

Fitz's heart beat furiously as he watched her. She was trembling all over, and a faint buzzing sound came from her direction.

"Don't you ever mention the word 'mustard' again in my presence," she warned in a slow, measured voice. "Not *ever!*"

Turning back to the cupboard, she opened it just far enough to stick her hand inside. She pulled out a red plastic squeeze bottle of ketchup and thrust it toward the boys. Then she slammed the cupboard shut again.

In the instant that the cupboard door was ajar, Fitz saw the shelf filled with ketchup bottles.

But at the same time, he spotted dozens of yellow plastic squeeze bottles on another shelf.

His eyes flew open. *Mustard!*

Why hadn't he thought of it before? Was *that* what they had been looking for all along? Plain old *mustard?* He felt his excitement growing.

That had to be the answer! he thought. Mustard was poisonous to the larvae! Why else would she forbid them to use it in the cafeteria and keep it hidden away?

Fitz made a flying leap, barreling into the cook and ramming his head into her stomach. Miss Larva sucked in her breath in surprise and sat down hard on the floor.

Fitz turned, ran across the room, and scrambled up onto the counter. He opened the cupboard door and grabbed a bottle of mustard.

"Don't touch that, you little *brat!*" screamed Miss Larva. She had clambered to her feet and was lunging for him.

Skittering across the counter out of her reach, Fitz plunged the yellow plastic bottle into his mouth and tried to squeeze.

But suddenly he felt weak. He tried to squeeze the mustard into his throat, but he couldn't.

"You are in our power," came the crackling voices from inside him. They sounded louder than ever before.

Then Miss Larva's hideous laughter drowned out the voices in Fitz's head.

"You think you're so clever, don't you?" she demanded. "Well, you aren't. Drop that mustard bottle this instant if you care about your little friend. I know all about her allergies. Especially her allergy to hamburger meat!"

To Fitz's horror the cook had Lexi in her grasp and was shoving a gigantic hamburger into her mouth. Lexi was gagging. Her eyes were open wide with terror.

Fitz knew he had no choice. There was only one way to save Lexi. And Brian. And himself.

Grasping the mustard bottle in both hands, he squeezed with all the strength he had left. It was the hardest thing he'd ever done—harder than running the cross-country course and then doing five hundred sit-ups. He squeezed even harder, gasping at the effort. The voices were chattering away rapidly inside his head.

Then he heard a gushing sound and felt the thick spicy mustard rushing down his throat.

Chapter

"Here! Drink this!" yelled Fitz. He pitched the mustard container to Brian.

Grabbing a second bottle, he pointed it toward Miss Larva.

She was struggling to hold on to Lexi and cram the hamburger into the frightened girl's mouth.

"Let her go!" he cried.

His hands were trembling. He was holding the mustard bottle straight toward her, but the cook was not going to give in easily.

Pitching the hamburger onto the floor, she ducked behind Lexi, using the girl for a shield.

"You'll never outsmart me," she croaked, backing slowly toward the door and dragging Lexi along with her.

Fitz tried to steady himself and aim the bottle so

that the mustard would strike Miss Larva.

A humming filled the air. It sounded as if an angry swarm of hornets were swirling through the room. Fitz looked around. If there were hornets in there, they were invisible.

Suddenly he could feel a rumbling deep inside his body. He shuddered uncontrollably as a giant wave of nausea rolled over him. His stomach was pitching and heaving.

The lumps on his side and leg were changing, too. They throbbed wildly. It was as if they were fighting against a force that was trying to suck them into his body.

The nausea was getting worse by the second. Fitz had never felt so sick in his life. He had a puckery feeling in the back of his mouth. He tried to swallow it away, but a putrid mass of vomit was rising in his throat, gagging him. And the sound of hornets was getting louder.

He raced for the sink, but he didn't make it. Opening his mouth as wide as he could, he started to retch. It felt as if his guts were pouring out. His breath was nearly choked off as slimy, foul-smelling larvae gushed out of his mouth and onto the floor.

There were purple larvae, green larvae, and black-and-yellow-and-white-striped larvae—just like the ones Fitz had seen in Miss Larva's lasagna pan. Only they were five times the size, and they were squirming and flopping around on the floor like fish out of water.

Beside Fitz, Brian was throwing up larvae, too.

Fitz held his nose. A terrible stench filled the room as the flopping larvae gradually stopped moving and died one by one.

The two boys clung together on wobbly legs. They panted with exhaustion.

From across the room Lexi let out a scream and bolted toward them. "Look out!" she cried. "She's behind you!"

Fitz whirled around. His mouth dropped open. He gasped and stared at a huge insect that was sitting on a counter across the room. It was nearly three feet long. Fitz had never seen anything like it before. It had the head of a horsefly and the body of a cockroach!

"Oh, my gosh!" he cried, pointing to the giant insect. "Look at that thing!"

Brian was as pale as a ghost. "It's Miss Buggy," he whispered.

Suddenly it was all perfectly clear to Fitz. "She's one of her own experiments! She turned herself into a mutant bug! And now she's—"

He stopped in midsentence. Out of the corner of his eye, he saw the huge insect moving slowly toward them. On its fly-type head were long cockroachlike antennae. The giant feelers waved crazily in the air as the bug advanced on the boys. The humming sound was coming from it, only now the sound was as loud as a jet airplane on takeoff.

"Watch it! She's coming after us!" Brian said in a trembling voice. "What'll we do? We can't get away! She's between us and the door!"

Miss Larva crept closer.

Fitz backed slowly away, bumping to a stop against the stove. He was staring into a mutant face that looked partly human and partly insect.

Suddenly the horrible bug reared up onto its back legs and waved its front legs menacingly at him. Its mouth opened wide, exposing razor-sharp pincers.

"Look out!" screamed Brian. "She's going to jump us!"

Fitz looked around desperately for the plastic mustard bottle. He had dropped it when the terrible nausea overcame him. Where was it!

Then he saw it. It was on the other side of the kitchen. He would have to run past Miss Larva to get it. Taking a deep breath, he darted through the foul mass of dead larvae until he spotted it, floating in the slime. He almost lost his balance, slipping and sliding across the floor.

Miss Larva turned toward Fitz, crouching to spring.

Fitz saw her jump into the air.

He stretched as far as he could, and his hand

closed around the mustard bottle. But just as he started to pick it up, it slipped away.

He grabbed for it again. This time he was able to grasp it. Whirling toward Miss Larva, he pointed it and squeezed with all his strength.

A golden stream of mustard arced across the room like a missile and hit the giant insect squarely in the mouth.

A human scream pierced the air when the mustard found its mark. Splashes of yellow filled the room like golden rain.

Fitz stared openmouthed at the huge bug as it crashed to the floor.

"Look!" cried Brian. "Look at her kick."

The bug had landed on its back. Mustard dripped from the side of its mouth. Its legs flailed for a few seconds as what was left of Miss Larva squirmed and squirmed, struggling desperately to turn onto her stomach and get back on her feet.

They watched in silence as her legs waved more and more slowly and gradually grew still. The hundreds of tiny eyes in her pupils turned milky and dull.

"She's dead," whispered Fitz. The three of them collapsed against each other in relief.

"We did it," Brian said in a weak voice. "We found the one thing that was poison to larvae."

Fitz nodded. "Yeah, and you'll have to admit that Miss Larva was pretty smart. She made her food so good that we all stopped eating at fast-food places. We hated our parents' cooking, too. There wasn't much of a chance that any of us would eat mustard and find out her secret—*that mustard was poison to larvae!*"

Suddenly he looked at Lexi. "Are you okay?" he asked her in alarm. "I mean, your allergies!"

"I'm fine," Lexi said proudly. "It was hard, but I didn't swallow anything."

"Wow," said Fitz in genuine admiration.

They set to work cleaning up the kitchen. They scooped up the dead larvae in the cook's lasagna pan and poured them down the garbage disposal. When the floor was mopped clean, they dragged Miss Larva outside and heaved her into the Dumpster.

"I guess that's about all we can do here," said Fitz as they headed back to the kitchen. "Let's pass out the poison to everybody else."

"Can we start with Sarah?" asked Lexi. "She's my best friend, and I'd really like to save her first."

Fitz grinned slyly at Lexi. "Let me do it. I'm good at making her puke."

Laughing, they loaded themselves down with the yellow plastic mustard bottles Miss Larva had hidden away so carefully and hurried off to find their teachers and friends.

Fitz looked at Lexi as she trotted along beside

him. She had been awfully brave when Miss Larva had her in her clutches. He was actually starting to like her in spite of the fact that she was a girl.

In fact, he thought, and smiled to himself, *I'm starting to like her a lot!*

About the Author

Betsy Haynes has written over fifty books for children, including *The Great Mom Swap*, the bestselling The Fabulous Five series, and the Taffy Sinclair books. *Taffy Goes to Hollywood* received the Phantom's Choice Award for Best Juvenile Series Book of 1990.

When she isn't writing, Betsy loves to travel, and she and her husband, Jim, spend as much time as possible aboard their boat, *Nut & Honey*. Betsy and her husband live on Marco Island, Florida, and have two grown children, two dogs, and a black cat with extra toes.